D.
AN ABORIGINAL ODYSSEY

DREAMTIME
AN ABORIGINAL ODYSSEY

Nigel Clayton

First published in Australia by Nigel Clayton in 2011

Copyright©Nigel Clayton, 2011, 2015

Printed by CreateSpace, an Amazon.com Company

The National Library of Australia Cataloguing-in-Publication data:

Nigel Clayton, 1963
Dreamtime: an Aboriginal Odyssey, 2nd Edition.
ISBN 978 0 9806585 8 3

1. Hiking--Australia--Fiction. 2. Dreamtime (Aboriginal Australian mythology) 3. Aboriginal Australians--Legends.

A823.4

Other Titles by this Author

The Long Road to Rwanda
Colonies of Earth
Fall of the Inca Empire
Inca Myths and Way of Life
The Templar: and the City of God
The Templar: and the Temple of Káros
The Templar: and the Cross of Christ
Underworld
Spacescape
Space Opera – Heaven and Hell
Tom of Twofold Bay
The Zuytdorp Survivors
Afghan
Afghan: The Script
Chivalry
The Caves of Hiroshima
Scourge
The Cure
Amazon
Furious George
This Pestilence, Bergen-Belsen
Templar, Assassination, Trial & Torture
Underworld
When the Virgin Falls
Kibeho: Original Script
The Kibeho Massacre: As It Happened
Non, Je Ne Regrette Rien - No, I (We) Have No Regrets
The Matter with Karen Mitchell

About the Author

Nigel joined the Australian Army in 1980 at age 17yrs and 2 months, and after completing training at Kapooka was whisked away to the School of Infantry, Singleton, New South Wales, Australia.

He served in the Infantry until injury forced a medical discharge upon him in 1996, after having served in Southeast Asia, 1982; PNG (with the AATPT), in 1990: during the Bougainville Crisis; and in Rwanda, 1995: known world-wide for the Kibeho Massacre which occurred on April 22nd of that year.

Serving in PNG was a major highlight within his career.

He was married in 1999 and has two children.

IN THE BEGINNING

Having created the world in all its adversity, the Great Father Spirit, known by many names, looked down from upon his seat in the sky-world and smiled. He was happy with all he saw, all that he had made; and all that which had been created was greater than good. But the land was missing something, and it suddenly occurred to the creator of all that there should be spawned from the dust of the ground a man and a woman, for you cannot have one without the other, as was the situation with all the animals created thus far.

There was man and woman to make, and magic available to mould them. From the dust of the ground grew both, each similar in appearance though being of different sex: and so created were a man to the north and a woman to the south.

The Great Father was pleased with what he had done and hence set each off on a short journey so that they would encounter one another.

Each travelled towards the other unsure of what they were. Neither had cast their eyes upon one of their own kind before. They each witnessed around them several creatures of different cast going about their business and what they saw was beautiful.

Suddenly, as each made progress on their venture, they saw each other come to view.

The man approached the woman.

"I am new to the land and have never seen another so vastly similar to myself," said the man.

"And I, too, have never seen another of similar cast to me, other than you," said the woman.

"You are different than me," said the man as he looked at her chest.

The woman cast her eyes downward. "And you are different than me."

An instinct took over the meeting, each filled with desire, each filled with a sense of togetherness.

"I am from the north," said the man.

"And I am from the south," said the woman.

"Together we shall make this land our own," said the man. "Will you be my wife and aid me in all things to come?"

"I shall, and together we will bring great joy to one another," agreed the woman of the suggested union.

And together they got along, making camp and forming the first clan, gathering food for which to eat, and always feeling as though there was still more to come in this life of theirs.

The woman looked at some of the creatures of the land around them, seeing for herself something that made her sad but brought her hope.

"I see that the creatures upon the land have young," said the woman. "I think it would be a good thing if we, too, could have young by giving birth to a baby."

"First we must make it," said the man. He cast his hands into a pool of water and wet the dusty ground. He formed clay and moulded it. It soon resembled a very small person but was lifeless.

"You must put this into your body and carry it with you, and when it is ready you will give birth," said the man.

"How?" queried the woman. "How do I do such a thing?"

"I do not know," said the man.

"Let us sleep on this thought," said the woman, "and when we wake on the morrow we can decide what to do."

"Very well," agreed the man. "A very good idea."

And so both the man and the woman went to sleep beneath their shelter not far from the fire, where the clay statue of the little person stood waiting, and it did not have to wait long.

The Great father Spirit, having heard what was going on, decided to grant the wish of both man and woman, and with his magic abilities he transferred the clay person from beside the fire and into the body of the woman.

When they both awoke they were at first concerned that the clay person was missing but it then came to pass that the woman felt movement within her. Within time she gave birth to the first child upon the earth and the man and woman was overjoyed.

And so the Great Father Spirit saw to it that there was plenty to eat for the population of men and women which was to come, and for all the creatures that currently existed, but he also knew it would take time.

And the law upon the land was that all men and women that were to be born unto the world were to refrain from eating meat, only the vegetation of all variety to be eaten in order to satisfy their hunger.

And so the Great Father Spirit sat back and watched.

NARAHDARN

The first man and woman lived happily over the pursuing months and with child their spirits rose, and they felt happy; but not always content.

Baiame, who was the Great Father Spirit, sensed that something was the matter one day when looking down upon his creations. He saw the woman looking up into the mosaic of a yarran tree which was a sacred tree.

The man come up and stood beside his wife with child. Baiame saw this as a moment to press upon them a matter of great urgency, for he was the creator and therefore provided the rules for life and death.

Baiame said to the man: "This tree is a sacred tree and upon it is something that has caught your eye."

"What is it?" asked the man.

"It is called honey and is made from bees: all things have names. You will now be known as Ber-rook-boorn, the one who carries the essence of man."

"Can we eat it?" he asked.

"No, it is forbidden," said Baiame.

"Then why did you make it?"

"I did not," answered Baiame. "The bees make it from the pollen of flowers. The honey is for them. And I should also warn you," continued Baiame, having noticed the stare of the woman upon the honey as it dripped from within the hive, "that I have placed Narahdarn, the bat, to watch over the honey which is for the bees. Narahdarn will be drawn forth if the honey is taken by you and then you will have to deal with Death."

"What is death?" asked Ber-rook-boorn."

"You mean to ask, who is Death," replied Baiame. "Death has the power to take your life if my laws should be broken, and there is nothing I can do about it. This tree belongs to Death; he is trapped within it which is why it is sacred. Do not allow him to escape. So the tree belongs to him, as the honey belongs to the bees, all of this in the same way that the name Ber-rook-boorn now belongs to you. Do not touch the honey," said Baiame once more and then disappeared from view.

It was several days later when the woman could stand it no more. The honey from the hive, hanging within the branches of the yarran tree, were dripping upon the ground and seemingly going to waste. It looked so delightful. So she grabbed her digging stick and pushed it into the hive, twirling the stick as she did so. The stick was soon covered in honey and she drew it out. Now placing it into her mouth her face lit up with a great expression of joy and as it did so there was a terrible screeching sound from atop the yarran tree.

Down came Narahdarn who planted himself upon a branch and hung there up-side-down.

"Who are you to take that which is sacred?" asked Narahdarn with a note of sarcasm attached.

"I am the wife of Ber-rook-boorn," she replied, nervously.

"Well, thank you," said Narahdarn. "For I am Death and come in disguise, and you have set me free, for me to take what form I wish. I like the look of your body, it provides much freedom in movement. I think I shall cast myself into similar proportions; but to be a woman with no name is not good enough, and so I shall be a man, and I shall be known as the Spirit of Death: or Yowie, if it should please your ear."

The woman was scared. "I have done a terrible thing."

"Yes, you have," replied Yowie. "For you have unleashed your terrible future to come; your end; and from this day forth your dreams will be filled with the terror of darkness, for death can now fall upon you at any time."

Narahdarn then waited not a moment longer and took to the sky and flew out of sight. The woman looked at the yarran tree and then saw something she could not believe. The tree was crying, tears of red gum falling down the trunk.

Death was now a part of life: life and death were like husband and wife.

THE SPIRIT OF DEATH

And time went by at a tremendous pace until one day the earth was home to many more clans than was thought possible, all descendants of Ber-rook-boorn and his wife.

The spirit of the Great Father woke, a feeling of urgency surging within him. He stood up from his bed of reeds and turned to come face to face with another.

And the Spirit of Death stood before the Great Father, their eyes locked, and the name of the Spirit of Death was Yowie: as you have been advised.

The Great Father looked upon the all prevailing Spirit of Death and feared it not, for what is to fear but fear itself. And so the Great Father stared into the blackness of lifelessness, this darker than coal-black figure of a monster like none other ever encountered before; and why was all of this? Because the Great Father had created life; great wonders and joy; he had created all that existed within the world; and if the created was a lifeless immortal then it could only be because it was a monster, created of mind and action, but not of purpose: an indispensable subconscious flaw within the framework of creation itself. The Great Father was the creator of all living things; of vegetation; of man and woman; and he had provided them with the laws of the land which were to be abided by for all eternity. But Yowie was cunning and shrewd.

"Do you know me, He who created all? Do you know who I am?"

"You are the Spirit of Death," replied the Father. "You are He who should be shunned. You are the reverse of life, opposed to living, a disfigured mirage; a shadow of the figment of imagination, the opposite of all good, and the most rudimental of all heinous decision, the oppressor in this world who will see the destruction of all that I have created: alas, Ber-rook-boorn and his wife have let me down."

Yowie stood there without a move as the Great Father expressed himself wholeheartedly; and now Yowie gave reply to the accusation.

"I am not that which you say I am, but more. I am the choice that men and women have in this life you have created for them. It is their will that they break your laws as they see fit, to suit themselves in their lives of hardship."

"If such is true then it is only through your manipulations."

For the first time during this short confrontation, Yowie looked both left and right, and then back again into the eyes of the Great Father.

"You created me, Father."

"No; not I. You were created through what will be known as temptation."

"Yes indeed, it is true," and a muffled laugh seemed to emanate from with the darkest of dark figure that stood before the Great Father. "But also, you moulded me in your dreams, where fear cannot be controlled: but you know this already. Your darkest fears created me from within when Narahdarn was placed to stand guard over the honey which was for the bees. You are a fool and have misjudged your man and your woman. You gave them child and they in turn have spurned you."

"I have nothing to fear—" started the Great Father, before being cut off in mid-sentence.

And the response given by Yowie was short and bitter to the ear as he concluded: "...but fear itself; and I am that, the living apparition of the only fear you can ever contemplate, and I come from your dream-state. I have been manifest from the deepest figments of your imagination."

The Great Father let out a wielding laugh to downplay what Yowie was seemingly instigating without realising the matter with the situation. "I have provided the living with the laws of the land; the laws of eternity."

"Laws are to be broken; have been broken," said Yowie.

"I do not believe you," replied the Great Father, hoping that the eating of the honey upon the yarran tree was the only incursion of man upon his laws.

"It is true," said Yowie. "You have provided a law by which all you have created in semblance of you are not permitted by law to eat of the flesh from any living thing, but I have seen to it that the law has been broken."

"That is not possible," defended the Great Father. "There is nourishment throughout the land; more roots, seeds, berries and fodder to feed a multitude of men and women."

"But the vegetation, of all you have created to feed the multitude, is dying, the men and women alongside, each sharing in the foreseeable future of all you have created."

"How; how can this be true?" and the sound that flowed from the lips of the Great Father were those of worry and concern.

"I have created a drought upon the land and vegetation right across it is dying, across the entire expanse of all you created except that upon my side of the river to the west and to the north. The men and women upon the earth are dying with it." Yowie paused with effect and then continued, Baiame in his silence requesting such continuance. "There was a man and a woman from beyond the Forbidden River who were starving to death, and the woman sought a way in which to feed her child. They broke your law and fed upon the flesh of a kangaroo rat that had made its way across the river and towards your people, the woman chiding the man to sup with her and the child; but one other refrained from eating, a man who appeared disgusted."

"So you see," insisted the Great Father, before hearing the remainder of the story. "My law stands, even in the face of desperation this single man has abided by my law; and now I shall fix the errors of their way, the error which these two adults have unwittingly performed."

"No need," said Yowie. "The man who refrained did run away from the couple with child and broke another of your laws by wading across the Forbidden River. In his urgency to get away from the evils of life another law has been broken, but I gave him aid."

"How?"

"He collapsed upon the earth on crossing the river within view of the couple, crying out as loud as can be that he was dying of starvation, their mouth still chewing on flesh; so I did swoop down from the tallest gum tree and stooped over his dying form. He drew in his last breathe and died there before my very eyes. I then took him to within my chamber, my quarters within the trunk of the gum tree, and cooked him. The fear I have created was heartfelt and all of the multitude have seen the vestiges of your law with concern to eating flesh; they have all seen the ruinations that will attend and attach themselves to a dying man through starvation; no one else will fear to come across the Forbidden River now, to fill their stomachs upon the greenery of all that I protect, or upon the wild and untamed animals that roam the land in plenty, and I shall provide further enticement in the form of edible meat ready to be slaughtered. And now, or so it seems, the multitude, as you so eloquently put them, are seeking a new way of life, walking about this land in search of nourishment and even coming across the Forbidden River to meet with their future: and death, of course, when it comes to visit. Of course, you must also be aware that when one law has been broken that more shall follow. Soon the land will be lawless."

"I shall put it to rights," said the Great Father. "I shall see to it that the errors of their ways are tuned back to the laws of the land. I shall see to it that all laws are embraced."

Yowie simply scoffed at the short speech and disappeared from view.

The Great Father was left in silence to ponder the situation, as dire as it was.

TO QUEST

Nalon [the source of the river] was sitting beside the fire of his camp in the lateness of night, having floundered in his sleep. He was considered an old man and had experienced several ceremonies during his life; ceremonies conducted to fine tune manipulations within the laws of the land as instigated by the elders of camps across all that the Great Father had created: but the changes were ordained by the many living as a clan, and clans seeking minor trade between one another. These fundamental changes in life did not alter the final command of each law: as a single leaf upon a flourishing tree, or a branch extending from the trunk, cannot affect its source, for the roots still remained the same. Ceremonies themselves, too, were rather artificial and void of purpose, for there was no reason that the men and women of the land to put great energy into ceremony, no current need to recall their histories through the flow of dance and music, because those living off the land were the first to live upon it, and they had no past to speak of: and no energy to perform them, for they were all very hungry.

The fire before him was spitting flecks of hot ash into its surrounds, more so than usual, and Nalon thought this was rather peculiar.

Nalon looked around to the entrances of the many shelters of the camp but not a soul was stirring from his or her place upon the mats or reeds that were employed as beds in which to sleep upon. He then returned his gaze back to the fire and became a little startled by what he saw now sitting there.

At first the figure was hard to see through the flames that leapt into the cold night air but as Nalon strained his eyes he began to see a shape form before him. It then stood up and smiled upon Nalon who reciprocated by standing and showing his teeth to the world. The figure then turned and walked off slowly, Nalon following with his eyes. The figure stopped, turned, and pursed with his lips that Nalon should follow him into the world, away from the light and warmth of the camp fire.

Some distance from the fire the figure stopped and awaited Nalon, who, seemingly hesitant at first, did finally arrive before the figure. The figure of the man before him held something in his hand. Nalon looked down at it and saw it was a shaped piece of wood from the coolabah tree and attached was cordage made from reeds. The figure before him began swinging the apparatus around and around, a circle created, and the light breeze created did disturb the surface of the wood which in turn created a voice which Nalon understood.

"I am happy to meet you, Nalon," said the Great Father as he whipped the wood of the coolabah tree round and round. "I am the Great Father Spirit, the creator of the world in which you live; creator of all living things, and the laws which bind life and existence; and that fire, too."

Nalon did not know what to do, how to greet the Great Father. "I believe it." Nalon was still quite stunned and looked at the wood as it was swung round in a constant circle, the voice of the Great Father coming from it. It was beautiful, like the music of the wind to the ear, like the echo from a deep cave or the canyons thereabouts.

"This is Gayandi and Gayandi is my voice," introduced the Great Father of his vocals. "If I was to speak to you as man to man, then you would not understand me. My Gayandi is my link, from spirit world to you."

"How do I make one?" asked Nalon.

"You will not need one, Nalon, as I understand all you say through the magic of my Gayandi as it moves through the air, but I shall give this to you as my gift before I leave and henceforth, from this day on, any time you wish to seek an audience with me all you need to do is swing this piece of coolabah wood as I am doing now, and an audience shall be granted, but be warned, only men shall here me from this day forth. Never shall a woman be trusted with the sight of my Gayandi, not after the breaking of one of my laws. Men may call it by its proper name, but any other must call it by the other name I have given it: bullroarer."

"It is a most wondrous sound..." said Nalon, closing his response early.

"You can call me Baiame, as does your clan, for you are all my special children; but know this; each clan knows me by a different name. As for my presence here... it is in regards to a broken law, broken, but not beyond repair, and you, Nalon, are the one who is to put things right," said Baiame.

"Put things right. What can you mean, Baiame?"

Baiame continued swinging his Gayandi as though no effort at all. "You must attend an urgent matter on my behalf, carrying my Gayandi wherever you go. You must walk about this great land I have created and put to right the laws of the land, and see to it that my laws are forever sealed within the fate of men and women of the present and future generations."

Nalon did not question the command from Baiame and simply nodded his head once. "I shall do as you say, Great Father, but what if I am to lose my way, or become fatigued; what If I am to stumble upon this great task you have set before me; after all, I am but an old man?"

"I shall guide you through the use of my Gayandi, and your age shall not weary you," said Baiame, and silence faltered the tide of conversation momentarily. "This is a visit upon you that cannot be afforded without a price and due to my incursions upon this land I have forfeited a deal, not in my favour, to the Spirit of Death, whose name is Yowie. It is therefore imperative that you know he will be about."

"The Spirit of Death has a name?"

"Yes, Nalon."

"And his name is Yowie; the one so named who resides across the river, upon the land of plenty. I saw it in my dreams."

"It is the land of plenty for those creatures that reign upon it, just like men and women reign upon the land saturated with sustenance on this side of the Forbidden River. But the sustenance is dying for Yowie has seen to it that the heat of the sun is scorching the land – the sun has been defiled. Many camps not dissimilar to yours have crossed the Forbidden River is search of food, breaking the laws of the land; and the scorching of the earth will soon fall upon you and your kin as it has others, the forests of swamp and wood turning to desert as the wind carries the heat ever towards the rising of the sun. You will see a desert forming on this side of the river, but on the reverse there is much life and greenery. It is the work of Death and his heinous act is spreading. Far into the day where the sun disappears at night is further desert and calamity."

"This is a bad day," said Nalon, "and it must be remembered so that your laws can be spared their annihilation."

"Gayandi has been made from the wood of the coolabah tree: hence forth I shall give purpose to your histories by forming a rudimentary word from the wood, and the memory of all history shall be recalled through a ceremony called corroboree. Remember your histories through the act of these."

And Nalon saw within his head the formation of dust and sound, and he knew immediately how to conduct a ceremony through corroboree.

"I shall let my people know," said Nalon. "I shall speak to the members of the camp and explain it all."

"Seek only an audience with your chief. Tell him you must seek justice in the world, and above all, you must depart immediately, for Yowie will not wait."

"I shall," said Nalon, "but before I do... can you answer me these two questions: where does fire come from, and why me, an old man?"

"The first is from Yhi, the goddess of the sun – not the sun itself. It is a power which is gifted to men in order to keep warm when times turn cold; it is given and must not be let go, for once it is out it is out. As to the other: I need a man of age, of maturity, who will not be swayed from the road, whose mind is set upon the way; who cannot be swayed by the treachery of women. Those are the answers. But there is one last thing before I depart; the key to your success is to come from observation. Observation is the key, to see how each clan accepts the laws, how each changes any given law to meet their own needs. See and hear all you can and learn all there is to learn. Through observation you will attain a greater understanding. And now I must be gone."

And as Baiame faded from view his voice could be heard: "Seek the yarran tree, wipe its tears away and give forgiveness to the wife of Ber-rook-boorn, for only man-spirit can fix what has been broken; but do not repeat this for any other to hear for Death may be listening."

Nalon then commenced what had been requested of him.

And Nalon had carried out his task well, advising the elder of all that needed to be advised.

THE JOURNEY BEGINS

The elder, who was chief, who had delivered judgemental conditioning upon Nalon and his existence, was stunned.

"It is hard to believe that Baiame should allow this to happen," said the chief, whose name was Apari [father].

"I do not know the whole story, but the Yowie must be stopped," said Nalon. "The laws must be protected. I have been given a task by Baiame, the Great Father Spirit, who is known by many different names, and shall work towards his goals."

"I must admit that I understand very little of this, Nalon, but I see there is great merit and honesty within you."

They both looked now, out across the Forbidden River and towards the new land of plenty, where wild animals roamed free. Clan after clan were moving into the heartland of the carnivores and herbivores, and Nalon knew that many animals in turn would cross the Forbidden River into the land of the clans.

The sun was commencing to dawn upon the day, the night sky starting to colour, bringing light and joy to the world. Nalon and Apari looked up at a passing cloud as it moved towards the rising sun. They then looked down at the river, which appeared like a scar, flowing between the two adversely different masses of land, dressed in hues of green and dying vegetation, but full of beauty.

"Are you sure you have not been dreaming?" asked Apari.

"No; no dream; and this is certainly no time to dream," said Nalon. "The day is almost upon us."

"Yes, you are right," agreed the chief. "Dreamtime it is not, and now it is time for you to go walking about."

Nalon looked up at nothing as a blank glaze fell across his face. "Dreamtime is not a state which is drawn from sleep, but the history of creation and the laws that bind it."

"That is beautiful," said Apari. "I see now why you have been chosen."

Nalon checked his waist belt made of reeds from which hung the Gayandi and then he checked it, too.

"Your walkabout will be an adventure like none other has ever experienced," said Apari. I wish you well, and I hope that you have little need to use the Gayandi."

"I, too," agreed Nalon. "And one other thing; if speaking of me whilst I am gone, of telling stories, say nothing of my Gayandi, for women are not permitted to see it or call it by its real name. Women are only to utter the word bullroarer and I know not why."

Nalon smiled now as it was time to part. "I am leaving now, to go walkabout: and from this day the word walkabout will become tradition, for it is the way that marks our sacred existence and makes a man of a child, and it replenishes the sacred existence of our laws to full purpose and fruition."

"You are great, Nalon," said Apari.

"I speak the words as provided me; a gift from the Great Father Spirit."

Apari could see it was now time for Nalon to depart. "I wish you well, Nalon," said the chief of the clan who knew the Great Father Spirit as Baiame. "Good fortune to you and your adventure. We will remember you. Your actions merit great reward, and as you are upon a quest as warranted by Baiame himself then you too shall be remembered, and your name shall be sacred within our clan."

"Is it not disrespectful to remember me in such a sacred way when it is Baiame who is sending me upon this great adventure?"

"Baiame voiced the laws of the land and you are to see them saved and sewn. There is no disrespect." said Apari. He then looked into the brightening sky-world and concluded with: "Let Baiame strike me down and turn me to clay if I am wrong."

Nothing happened.

"We shall remember you, Nalon."

Nalon smiled. He had been given a great honour.

No further word was necessary and Nalon stepped down the embankment and towards the Forbidden River. He looked across it and saw a gum tree standing there. For a moment, so solitary in existence that it could not possibly exist, Nalon thought he saw a shadow; but the sun was not yet high enough to form such a thing across the expanse of land about him.

He shook the vision from his mind and stepped into the waters of the Forbidden River and waded across with a little difficulty encountered.

Nalon stepped out onto the opposite side of the river and turned once more to see the elder of his camp but he was disappointed, for the elder was already gone. And Nalon had to consider that it was possible that he would never be remembered.

EVIL UNLEASHED

Yowie was standing before the entrance of a cave and within it was who he sought: none other than Marmoo, the Spirit of Evil.

Yowie wasn't alone in the world and for every ounce of good that was created a superior amount of evil ensued to counterbalance it.

"Marmoo!" screeched Yowie. "Marmoo; are you in there!"

A stirring could be heard and a growl from deep within erupted from the dark depths.

"Marmoo, it is I, Yowie."

Marmoo listened hard and recognised the voice of Death, and was unmoved by the interruption from the slumber he'd sought.

"I have had a busy night," said Marmoo. "Come back later."

"But this is a matter of urgency," insisted Yowie, "and concerns the Great Father Spirit.

Marmoo startled Yowie then but appearing suddenly at the entrance to the cave in which he slumbered. "The Creator: He is not great to me, not by any means."

"You hate him with all your heart," said Yowie, presenting a sly grin.

"I have no heart," corrected Marmoo. I am hollow within."

"No, you are full; full of hate," insisted Yowie.

"The Creator was wrong to have cast you, Yowie," said Marmoo. "I think you will be his undoing, in the end."

"No; I am only death," said Yowie. "But wherever I get the opportunity I shall see death delivered, with or without good cause. I may cast the stone but the striking down must be the result of another."

"Tell me, Yowie; what have you done?"

"I have seen to it that a law of the land was broken, but not through fault of my own," said Yowie, fidgeting slightly. "I simply... nudged it along, just a little."

"And so what do you want of me?" asked Marmoo.

"The more the multitudes of the... you know who."

"Huh!"

"The more they crave for food the more they shall break the laws of the land. They feed upon the shrubs, roots, flowers and grass, like the animals that roam wild upon my side of the Forbidden River. If you could somehow see to it that the food source was... strained, then the clans would have all the more need to break His laws."

"I see," said Marmoo, clearly thinking, considering it hard. "I see; yes indeed. And I think I have an answer."

"Oh, so quick you are, Marmoo, with your depravity. I like it."

"I shall send forth a monstrous army," said Marmoo.

"An army," said Yowie, seemingly disappointed. "More people upon the land? Please; no more."

"Not people, Yowie, but a cast of... I shall call them, insects."

"Insects?" queried Yowie.

"Yes," decided Marmoo. He turned on the spot and looked into the dark depths of his cave and held up both his hands, outstretched his arms, closed his eyes, and breathed a few incomprehensible words of incantation. And then he opened his eyes and lit his face with a smile as a buzzing noise grew louder and louder from within the dark depths of his home.

Yowie looked yonder into the darkness as the sound grew louder and louder, and even he, one who is dead, did give a shudder as the air all around him vibrated with feverish ferocity. And then it erupted, an enormous mass, like a dark and menacing cloud which was alive.

Yowie then looked towards the foot of the cave and saw the same, but the great mass was moving, individual parts scurrying along on feet: some had eight legs, others one hundred.

And so the great mass of life flew over the standing form of Marmoo, or trumpeted along past in quick action beside him upon the ground, to do the bidding of their master.

Yowie stepped back and watched in amazement, and Marmoo opened his mouth to give introduction. "This is my army, one that shall devour the world of all flowers, berries and all other fodder too numerous to mention. Not even the bark on trees will be spared. The army shall roam the land, Yowie, and devour everything in its path, whether on ground or in the air at the end of branches. The army shall fly and walk, sting and sup, sing and dig, hide and scurry, and above all else they shall multiply and multiply until they number millions of times more than the number of men and women created by our adversary."

And Yowie was also pleased beyond contemplation, but as the swarms upon swarms of insect life made its way towards the lush green acres that were left beyond the Forbidden River, Nalon was watching, looking upon them from behind a rock formation.

ON WINGS OF FORTITUDE

Nalon was horrified by what he saw: the swarms of vegetation-eating scavengers. He retreated to a safe distance and then spared not a moment of time and untied the Gayandi from his waist belt made of reeds. He allowed it to fall to its full length upon its cord and began swinging it round and round. The Gayandi sang and offered its voice to the wind, penetrating the world.

The Great Father Spirit heard the call and appeared out of thin air, standing there before his champion, Nalon.

"You seek an audience," announced the Great Father.

"There is a great urgency that has made itself present," stammered Nalon, almost uncontrollably. "I saw an army, with my own eyes, a mass of cloud which was alive, eating everything in its path."

The Great Father looked up into the sky-world and closed his eyes, Nalon looking on. The Great Father tilted his head this way and that and then slowly turned towards the sound of munching jaws upon flowers, grasses, and trees.

"This way, Nalon; follow me."

And amidst the growing swarms the Great Father lead Nalon down a small decline and onto the open expanse of low and undulating ground.

"Here we shall do battle," announced the Great Father.

"How; how is it to be done?" asked Nalon.

"Watch and you shall see."

The Great Father then cast his deep and rumbling voice to the sky-world and the ground began to vibrate, and from the depths of the earth came a shudder and great tremor. A cliff face was then born from the bowls of the earth, and was soon to tower over the land around them to dominate the scenery for as far as the eye could see.

Suddenly the tremors born of the earth subsided and again the great voice from within the Great Father did make a command of the sky-world. A mass of white smoke seemed to come out of nowhere, like puffs of smoke ballooning into great balls of fluffy white, filling the sky until all the blue above the earth had turned into a fantastic mass of cloud. And it commenced to darken, and lightening appeared.

Nalon was scared and cowered behind a large gum tree for the vibrating earth was one thing to put up with, but now the sky itself was on fire with great streaks of white lights emanating from the blackness above.

The clouds above suddenly erupted in a downpour of rain. Nalon could only look up in wonder as he held his palms up to the sky, the droplets of water falling upon his naked palm.

"It is water from sky-world," said Nalon.

"And look yonder," commanded the Great Father. "I shall call it a waterfall."

The rain from sky-world was falling so fast and heavy that a stream was born upon the plains now in existence upon the cliff, and was falling over the cliff and into a hollow upon the undulating ground, and many insects died as they drowned in the water.

"Look, Nalon," and the Great Father pointed. "Behind the curtain of water that falls from the ground above are hidden great masses of plant life and blossoms, each seed within the fine fabric of vegetation able to provide a further emergence of life and source of food for the men and women of this world."

"But the army of creatures so small will devour the seeds before they have a chance at life," said Nalon.

"And so I shall create an enemy for these creatures so small and cumbersome," said the Great Father, "an enemy that will devour them in turn, day after day, keeping them in check for all eternity. What the waterfall fails to protect, the other I create shall provide solace."

And the Great Father clapped his hands together and from behind the water fall erupted a bird of magnificent plumage, so beautiful that Nalon had never seen anything like it before in his entire life. "From the flowers behind the protection of the waterfall comes life, and I shall call it a lyrebird."

And immediately so the magnificent bird commenced to eat its fill of the army of insects in its midst. And then another bird appeared, and again another.

"But as the army surrounding us is made of many varieties, I too must combat this with great imagination."

The Great Father clapped his hands together one more time and from the waterfall burst hundreds upon hundreds of birds of different sizes, thousands of them filling the air and devouring the enemy in full sight.

"And where the destructive army shall go, the savours of this land I have created shall do their duty."

Nalon stood with his mouth wide open. "What you have created is a wondrous thing."

"They are birds," said the Great Father. "And... I hear a message upon the wind... The army is made up of insects. And where the wind carries the name of this heathen, so I shall whip up a wind to help carry them to their death."

With further great calamity felt upon the soul of Nalon a wind came out from nowhere to accompany the rain, stinging at his bare flesh and to carry the insects and birds alike towards the open sea and further afield upon the world so large.

Nalon clutched at his own body, the cold growing, his bones feeling the pressures of the good against evil.

The Great Father saw the pain in the eyes of Nalon and commanded with an almighty gesture of his hands that the world should return to calm, and as his hand shot into the air the wind did stop, the rain ceased to fall, and the cloud above broke up into little pieces and faded away.

"How are you, Nalon?"

"I shall be alright soon enough; once my bones have warmed themselves sufficiently."

"Good," said the Great Father as he looked around.

The attack of the insects upon the vegetation of the land had subsided dramatically and birdlife could be seen flying here and there, catching the insects within their beaks and eating them.

"What I have done cannot be changed. The birds are now here forever."

"But they are needed," added Nalon.

"And the weather is now unstable; it shall come and go. Clouds will gather, rain shall fall, and water will fill the low ground and change the look of the land for all time."

"And it looks beautiful," finished Nalon.

The Great Father smiled. "My job is done, for the moment, but that monster Yowie will return to cause more pain and death upon my people. You must do all you can to warn all others of his presence, of the way in which I am changing the world for the better."

"I shall, Great father Spirit," said Nalon. "And thank you for coming so quickly."

"We shall work together, Nalon, me and you, but it shall not be an easy victory. I shall also order one more creation to impart good fortune upon the land. I shall call this the pygmy-possum and it shall help eat the insect armies of this world till none remains."

And no sooner had he arrived and the Great Father Spirit had disappeared. It was then that a great flash of light erupted from the sky and struck the ground, a long, long way off, into the place where the sun went to sleep at the end of each passing day. It was here that the pygmy-possum was created.

THE BORA CEREMONY

Over the coming days Nalon did learn many things; amongst all was a power that he had to make changes which affected his life, for the better. Where he built a camp fire, a flame would be procured very easily; where food was sought a bountiful supply of berries, seeds and bulbous roots made themselves available; and where shelter was sought he would find large leafs, concave cavities in rock formations, or fallen logs ready to lay beneath to shelter him from the rain; but for all the small things that appeared out of nowhere to aid him along in his journey there was no aid given in regards to where to look for law-breaking clans.

It was as though the Great Father Spirit was providing him aid, but it was selective.

Nalon had come across an area thick with many trees where a canopy overhead made it too difficult to see the sky. He thought how beautiful it all seemed, all quiet and surreal when his thoughts were suddenly disturbed by a voice at his flank.

"Who are you?" asked a voice.

Nalon looked and saw a young man – or elderly child – standing before him, a spear in his right hand slowly lowered.

For a reason unknown to Nalon when he opened his mouth he said: "I am Nalon, a wirinum [medicine man] from afar."

"A wirinum?" queried the man.

"Yes," stammered Nalon, lacking the confidence of one so able.

"A wirinum, travelling alone in the forest?" the man said, once more the doubt upon his voice implying a lie. And then: "You have come for the gathering."

"Yes, I have," said Nalon, and to convince the man to his front added: "I am of the Alkira [sky] clan." And Nalon considered that that name was as good as any other to masquerade his reason for being there.

"I have never heard of them," stated the man.

"We are from the far side of the Forbidden River but the others of my clan are reluctant to pass this way. I heard of the gathering, upon the wind, and it was the good judgement of the elders that representation should be forwarded."

"Very good," said the man. "My name is Kulan [a possum]. I am from the Madhi clan. There are others at the gathering from Du-mer, Wahn, and Biamul; and several other less important clans that are yet to find their way."

"Find their way?" queried Nalon.

"As you yourself seek prosperity from hunting as I do today, to sup on the flesh of living things in the wild."

"This is what I seek," lied Nalon. "Can you show me the way to the site of the gathering, Kulan?"

"It would be my honour," replied Kulan, with a smile. "Please, it is this way."

Nalon followed Kulan in silence and it wasn't long before the voices of the gathering could be heard and before Nalon knew it he was stepping out onto a cleared area within the forest, but the canopy was untouched, so, although at ground level much ceremony and celebration could be performed, there was not much light from the sky above to shine upon the scene of jubilation.

Nalon could see that there was a cleared area, a circle upon the ground cleared to represent the sky-world. Nalon considered this and thought it would please the Great Father Spirit, but the people about seemed to be making far too much noise for what must be a special occasion, men and women alike laughing out loud and telling funny stories to one another.

"Please, Nalon," said Kulan. "As a wirinum I ask that you help yourself in these festivities and make introduction to others of your title. I see several over there," and Kulan pointed with his lips, pursing them. "But I must attend my own chief and seek forgiveness for coming back empty handed."

"Of course," said Nalon. "I understand," and Kulan walked away.

Nalon stepped over to several wirinum of the other clans and listened intently to what was being said, and a deep and heavy voice cast itself out over the gathering of clans.

"Listen to me, all of you." It was Matari [a man] of the Du-mer. "We are here to see young men join with initiation, the first for us in this new land. The Great Father Spirit will be watching us from sky-world and hence we must see fit to justify the changes to His laws; but we must seek assent from Him."

The wirinum from the Madhi clan, known as Nowra [black cockatoo], yelled out: "Ah, be quiet, Matari. We know why we are here, and we seek no justification. We change the laws because they mean nothing to us anymore. We seek the New Way." He was tall and his skin was as dark as night.

"Does the New Way include chastising young men seeking initiation?" questioned Matari.

"How dare you question our reasons for such chastisement," yelled Nowra. "We seek no praise and do as we find just in this New World by enacting the laws of the New Way."

Matari looked at all the surrounded him, those to be imitated entering the bora circle. "This shall not be the way inherited by my clan."

"But it will be for mine and many others!" yelled the wirinum of Madhi.

Suddenly, and quite feverishly, Nalon was filled with great distaste and venom, and burst the banks of his silence by erupting in vocal assault upon the wirinum of the Madhi. "Listen to me, all of you. I am Nalon, he who acts on behalf of the Great Father Spirit, and it is He who finds great dishonour in the way you are treating his laws."

"Who are you really? Speak! I demand it!" yelled Nowra, the wirinum of Madhi.

"I am he who acts on behalf of the Great Father!" challenged Nalon as he uplifted his hands to skyward and gave clear address to sky-world. "Let the Great Father Spirit see to damnation this heinous act of treachery upon his circle of clan togetherness, where each and every one of you has come to the bora ceremony and acted out in unacceptable behaviour."

The wirinum of Madhi burst out in laughter as other of neighbouring clans seemed to shudder and sink away, cowering behind trees and one another. "You are not invited," said Nowra. "Not only this but it is fact that none here know of you."

"I have been chosen," voiced Nalon, "and you shall be punished for breaking the law of the one who resides in sky-world."

The brow of Nowra squeezed in and furrowed, a tightness forming around his mouth as anger grew inside; and as the young men to be initiated, and those men and women spectators of other clans watching the ceremony, stood and stared openly in aghast, Nowra stepped towards Nalon to see conflict ensued between them.

Nalon, not fearing reprisal of any description, unleashed Gayandi and let it fall to its fullest extent. Nowra seemed to miss this action but he saw what happened next.

Nalon started to turn Gayandi in circles, faster and faster; and a voice penetrated the bora ceremony for all to hear.

"You have violated my laws by killing, and by eating the flesh of animals. You have forsaken the bora ceremony, one which is sacred upon this land for as far as the eye can see, and you have acted in an insulted, manipulative, and unacceptable manner."

Nowra had stopped dead in his tracks, a look of deep and penetrating fear over taking his expression of anger, and all those men and women watching from the Madhi clan could sense that this was not a good day. Kulan also looked deeply into the eyes of Nalon and felt the fear grow within him for tempting the wraith of the Great Father.

And the voice of the Great Father Spirit continued: "The young men here are to be initiated, not to be ridiculed in front of clan members; but you, the Madhi, have tempted me too far. This world is vast, my constant presence upon it quite impossible; this is why you have wirinum to care for the laws within the clans so bountiful, but you, the Madhi, have lost your way.

"All here, at this place I so name Googoorewon [place of trees], shall bear witness. You! The Madhi! Your snarls of heinous and torturous laughter are not signs of men and women, but signs of beasts and nothing more," and in final ferocity the Great Father Spirit cast a great magic upon the Madhi and all of them, as one, fell to their hands and knees.

They wriggled and stretched, twisted and contorted, and above all... they changed. A tail grew from between their hind quarters, ears extended up and out from their heads, their arms became legs on which to stand and before all present the Madhi, to the last, were turned into dingoes.

They snapped and snarled as their final form took shape and as each turned his and her head to look upon other members of the gathering, those from other clans, they did run off into the forest as the scared creatures they were.

Nalon simply stood there and slowed his action, Gayandi coming to a halt and then quickly folded away.

A woman took a hesitant step towards Nalon and help out an outstretched hand, as though attempting to take the bullroarer. She faltered and pulled her hands back in. She looked Nalon in the eye.

"It is the sacred voice," said Coorah [a woman]. "The voice from the bullroarer... it was the Great Father Spirit."

"Yes, it was," certified Nalon.

"My name is Coorah. I had heard a story of the sacred voice from the Great Father Spirit. Where we come from we call this sacred representation of His voice, tjurunga."

"Then so be it," agreed Nalon. "Bullroarer it is, but tjurunga shall be its sacred calling to all women."

"Thank you for this great gift," said Coorah.

"The unveiling to you of the voice was not of purpose, but let us breathe purpose into it. Let me ask you," started Nalon as those around them stood in silence, "where is your wirinum; the voice of your clan?"

"He was killed."

"Killed?"

"By a beast," said Coorah.

"What manner of beast is it that killed a wirinum of the people I created," said Nalon, forgetful that he was a representative of Baiame, not the Great father Spirit himself.

"Are you the Great Father Spirit?" asked Coorah. "If so, who commanded the voice of the tjurunga?"

"I am His representative," and giving a short pause to be struck down dead, Nalon waited; but he remained as he was. It was therefore a justified representation. "I speak for Him; all that He has created, I have created. I carry his tjurunga, known to men by another name, and speak for Him. Now tell me, Coorah; what manner of beast did kill the wirinum of your clan."

"We saw a great flash of light come from the sky," said Coorah. "We thought it was... you."

Nalon recalled seeing the same flash of light, and recalled what the Great Father had said about being called upon: that each time he made visit upon the earth, Yowie would be awarded a prize, and to be more specific, 'due to my [the Great father Spirit] incursions upon this land I have forfeited a deal, not in my favour, to the Spirit of Death, whose name is Yowie. It is therefore imperative that you know he will be about'.

"What do you know of this 'flash of light'?" asked Nalon, pressing for valuable information.

"Our elders and chief dispatched scouts to reconnoitre the land and they came back without our wirinum, whose responsibility it was at the time to investigate all strange phenomena. When they returned to our camp they reported seeing several beasts upon the land."

"Can you tell me something of these beasts?" asked Nalon.

"The name they gave the one that killed our wirinum is burna-korra [fabricated name for a palorchestes], an herbivore like us, scoffing down all that was ours to eat. But there is more. They saw another; they called it mallee-akana [fabricated name for a diprotodon]. What manner of creatures are these that eat what is ours? Can you see now why we wish to gain sustenance from the flesh of animals in order to survive? If these monsters of the land take all that is ours then we shall starve."

"How many of these creatures did your men see?" asked Nalon.

"One of each, but where there is one there is sure to be more."

"Two cannot eat what is for all the men and women of this land; it is too much," said Nalon unconvinced.

"They are huge. A mallee-akana is twice as long as a man and as tall, and the burna-korra had claws as long as my hand: was half as large as a mallee-akana if not larger with a long snout on the front of its face."

"These are devil creatures," admitted Nalon.

"We cannot survive on a handful of grass and berries left behind by such large... monsters," finished Coorah with effect.

Nalon did not know what to do and so stepped back from the bora circle upon the ground where young men stood and watched as he removed himself. "I shall return shortly; meanwhile you shall sit and sip some flavoured water."

Nalon had stepped from, what appeared to be, a matter of disgrace. He knew not what to do, there were no answers in his head.

With great reluctance he took Gayandi from his waist belt and swung it round in circles and as though by magic the Great Father Spirit appeared one more time before him.

"You have represented me well before the clans, but now I find myself in your midst but once again. What urgency presents itself that I should be required?"

"A great calamity, Father," started Nalon. "There exist too many hard decisions to be made."

"But you must make them, Nalon," said the Great Father. "My voice was called upon by you at the bora ceremony and again now. This means that Yowie will have two acts to play out; two vengeful errands to perform upon all I have created."

"I am sorry, Father, but I need answers," insisted Nalon.

"Very well," said the Great Father reluctantly. "But from this day forth you must learn to make the decisions for yourself. You must learn from my judgement, and represent me to the full. So tell me what you know."

And so Nalon explained all that there was to explain in regards to Coorah, the beasts, and the foreseeable struggle to survive.

And the Great father Spirit did not disappoint though decisions made were not to his satisfaction.

"Go and do your deed, Nalon, pass on my message as though born of my lips," said the Great Father.

"Yes, Father; and when next you hear me calling with your Gayandi, please ignore it, for I shall instil good cause within the mind of men by offering them commands void of your presence, and this action will deny Yowie a small measure of vengeance upon you but still provide confidence to the clans."

Nalon returned to the gathering where several dingoes foraging nearby amongst the forest litter upon the ground did run off quickly.

Nalon stepped into the bora circle. "All listen to what must be," he commanded, and everyone came to see what the matter was.

"Judgement has been made and here is the judgement, but it is only for the men to hear what I am about to say, for the laws of the Great Father Spirit are for the ears of men and men alone, as it is for women to surrender themselves to the work of women. All women are to gather their belongings and move towards where the sun goes to sleep at night, taking good care to collect food for each of their clans. Gather grass, roots, berries, flowers, and all other good food to be found, and await the return of your men, for there will be no boys to be seen here after the ceremony which is about to be performed. Women have their sacred ceremonies and so too, the men shall have theirs; this is the law."

The women of all the clans gathered their things and moved off into the dying night; and before the sun rose, the ceremony would be over with, and food enough gathered for a good meal to be consumed.

The young men who had presented themselves at ceremony, for the initiation into manhood, stood awaiting their ordeal. The wirinum, elders, chiefs and men of all the clans remaining waiting to be given guidance as they looked upon those within the bora circle.

Nalon took the Gayandi from its place upon his hip and twirled it round and round, and the voice, now from within Nalon, echoed out through it to the ears of all those that listened.

"It is herald that the Spirit of Death has come to cause suffering upon you, my people, and as such it is my duty to award you a new law by which to combat this disaster. It is not my way to change that which had been cast of the soil of the earth but it is my way to ensure the safety of all men and women.

"Those young sons wishing to walk the earth as real men shall suffer by the hand that feeds them by having your two front teeth knocked out with stones, have your flesh cut by the blade of the wirinum, and suffer the pain of this world. You shall then walk beside your fathers and learn to kill at the hunt those beasts that take from you and your children, namely those created by the Spirit of Death, this now being permitted by law, to kill for meat with the weapons forged by you. But no other meat shall be eaten."

And the Gayandi slowed in motion and came to a stop.

The wirinum looked at each of the other, all clan representatives slowly taking up stones and knives, moving forward into the confines of the bora circle, to inflict the pain and suffering that a son must endure in order to become a man: and not a single one disappointed.

The clans from across the land were now permitted to eat meat but the laws of ceremony and life must be ensured and so Nalon continued with his odyssey.

THE FIRST PARROT

At the site of the Allora [place of the swamp] clan, was a people busy at task, for there was to be a wedding on the morrow: Bullai-bullai was to wed Beereeun.

Bullai-bullai stood opposite Weedah, a man who was a great hunter, the best that the clan had to offer. Forever the hunter seemed to be away on his solitary hunting trips, bringing home the meat that the clan needed so much in order to live and grow.

"Weedah, oh Weedah," softly spoke Bullai-bullai as she looked at Weedah. "What am I to do? I am to wed Beereeun tomorrow afternoon but I am so much in love with you."

Weedah was very careful and it was good that they were out of sight and unable to be seen by anyone of the clan. His hand brushed against her shoulders before falling away as he snatched a brief look over his own.

"And I love you, too," said Weedah with a smile, "but the wirinum has spoken and demanded a beautiful wife, and as you are the most beautiful... I cannot bear it," he finished with a tear falling from his eye.

"There must be something we can do," urged Bullai-bullai. "There must be something can be done."

"Yes; yes there is," responded Weedah as a great idea coursed through him. "We shall run away; far away from here."

"How," said Bullai-bullai, "when we are watched every moment of the day and night?"

"I am a hunter, the best of the clan, and to be so proficient I must spend time away from our camp. The clan know I am away from dawn till dusk on most days and tomorrow will be no different. If I remember correctly you also have a morning of collecting yams and roots for the ceremony. You shall meet them and go along, and when you see my signal you shall wonder off and meet me. That will give us at least half a day to put as much distance as possible between us and Beereeun."

"Yes," smiled Bullai-bullai, "and possibly even more, for Beereeun is as old in age as he is ugly to the eye, and he will put off searching till the following morning."

"I believe you are right," agreed Weedah, and so they formulated their plan of escape to commence on the morrow, when he was to go hunting and Bullai-bullai was to accompany the other women in search for yams and roots.

Nalon was making good progress and had turned away from his general advance and was in fact moving almost parallel to the Forbidden River, though at least half a day from it. It was an urge within, more than anything else, which forced him in this direction.

It was not long after first light when he stumbled across a camp in disarray with many hunters jumping here and there, picking up spears and water bags, preparing for what looked like a long journey. Suddenly he came face to face with the wirinum, Beereeun.

"Who are you? Questioned Beereeun, with a frown upon his forehead as he clutched hard upon the shaft of his spear.

"I am Nalon of the Alkira Clan, from the far side of the Forbidden River."

"What are you doing here at such a time as this? We are at urgent errand and so your presence here is either extremely coincidental or well-orchestrated."

"Why," asked Nalon. "What is the matter?"

"A hunter by the name Weedah has taken away with one to be my wife; her name is Bullai-bullai. Have you seen them?"

"No; no, I have not," answered Nalon.

Beereeun watched with much scrutiny the folds on the face of Nalon and could be the appearance of truth being spoken.

"I believe you," said Beereeun as several hunters drew up beside him. "Have you left your clan or are you on a mission of trading?"

"No," answered Nalon. "I am on a mission to see the laws of this land re-established, for many clans have lost their way. The Great Father Spirit wishes to see the laws resewn and forever custodial to our way of life, but has provided change where change is required and henceforth deemed it appropriate to eat the meat of animals; but only the meat of those created by Yowie, the Spirit of Death."

Beereeun could see that the hunters were now ready. "I must be off to search for my wife and her abductor, but you may join me and my band if you so desire; or you can wait here for my return. Either way I would like to hear more."

"I would be happy to attend," said Nalon, "and eager to learn new ways myself."

"Good," concluded Beereeun, "and on the way you can tell me of these creations you speak of."

And so Nalon told Beereeun everything there was to know of the burna-korra and mallee-akana.

It was late in the afternoon when Weedah and Bullai-bullai came upon the narrowest portion of the Forbidden River that Weedah knew of.

"This is it, Bullai-bullai; the crossing point I told you about," said Weedah as he pointed jubilantly across the way with his lips pursed.

"But the river," said Bullai-bullai. "It is moving too fast for me to cross. As a hunter you can perform such horrendous tasks as crossing rivers with great ease, but I; I cannot."

Weedah looked at the flow of the water and suddenly realised the truth of the matter.

"In fact," he said," I think I have overestimated my own ability. I think it will even be too much for me. It is the season where much water comes from far away and makes the crossing ever-more formidable."

"What shall we do?" asked Bullai-bullai.

"I do not know," replied Weedah who then looked up at the far side of the river.

What Weedah saw then took him rather by surprise, and pleasantly at that. There before him he saw a man in a canoe and he was paddling their way.

"Look, Bullai-bullai," pursed Weedah of his happiness. "I see a stranger who will soon be our friend, I am sure." Weedah lifted his left hand into the air, holding on fast to the spear in his right. He waved and waved and voiced his request. "Please; please help us. We are in need of crossing the Forbidden River."

The man came to a stop as his canoe hit the bank. He stood up and stepped from his dugout.

"Hello," he said, and as his eyes fell upon the glorious and beautiful features of Bullai-bullai, added: "I am Goolay-yali; how can I help you."

"I am Weedah and this is Bullai-bullai," said Weedah. "We wish to get across to the other side of the river."

"Most people want to come across this way," said Goolay-yali a little confused. "Why do you wish to go back across towards where the sun comes up when I hear there is much food to be had on this side?"

"We simply wish to see some friends, is all," lied Weedah, and Goolay-yali could see the lie in his face.

Bullai-bullai appeared to blush: they were not telling the truth. Gollay-yali thought to himself how he could make good fortune out of their misery.

"I can help you," said Goolay-yali, "But as you can see my canoe is only a small one, which I use for fishing. I can take you across but it can only be one at a time."

It was then that some shouting could be heard some distance from within the forest behind them and Weedah became urgent. He knew that if they were caught that he would be killed but Bullai-bullai spared, to live a life in torment.

"Please, take me across first and then return for Bullai-bullai," said Weedah.

"Certainly," said Goolay-yali, and to show he was on their side he added, "I am also short on time as I have another urgent errand to perform this day."

This made Weedah happy and he clambered aboard the small canoe without further ado.

Goolay-yali moved his canoe quickly to the other side of the Forbidden River and Weedah anxiously got out. Goolay-yali then left him there and returned to fetch Bullai-bullai. As his canoe hit the bank Bullai-bullai endeavoured to climb aboard.

Goolay-yali pushed her to the ground. "Where do you think you are going?"

"I must join with Weedah," cried Bullai-bullai. "We are promised to each other."

"But I have not seen a woman as beautiful as you for a long time," said Goolay-yali, "and I think you would do well to serve me for the rest of your life."

And although Weedah was sure of his and her fate, Bullai-bullai was not as confident and felt that Beereeun would see to her death. She had little choice, therefore, but to shed her tears and surrender to capture.

Bullai-bullai looked across the river and could see that Weedah was extremely anxious to be with her but the river was too strong. Further shouting was heard once more behind her but it appeared to be moving away. She turned to look Goolay-yali in the face.

"First you shall gather much wood and build me a fire," ordered Goolay-yali, wishing Weedah to see how he commanded her to do his bidding, "and then you shall cook me a meal fit for a chief."

It was growing dark and the birds, so new to the world, started singing triumphantly a goodnight to the sun, and as the fish upon the fire seemed ready to eat Bullai-bullai bent down to gather its flesh so that Goolay-yali could eat of it.

Goolay-yali leant ever forward and Bullai-bullai, feverishly ignorant of the hot coals within the fire, scooped up a handful of ash and threw it into the face of Goolay-yali.

He screamed and screamed, waking Weedah up from his staggered slumber, and danced upon the spot where his hands raced to usher the ash from his scolded flesh. Bullai-bullai got to her feet and abruptly turned upon her heals in readiness to get to the canoe and make good her escape when she collided with Beereeun, his hunters behind him.

"I have you now, Bullai-bullai," said Beereeun. "I have been watching you and Goolay-yali for quite some time, allowing you to fester in your misery, but now I think you have learnt a good lesson, that you cannot trust anyone except me."

"But I do not love you," blurted Bullai-bullai.

"That does not matter to me," said Beereeun. "You are sure to grow to love me, and I shall provide you a message for eternity, to be reminded of your poor judgement and previous choices." And within the flash of lightening which struck the ground in an enormous thunderous strike, Weedah was consumed in vapours of misty white smoke and disappeared from view.

"What have you done to him?" sobbed Bullai-bullai as the tears flowed freely down her cheeks. "What have you done to my Weedah?"

"Why, he is up there, my sweet," said Beereeun as he pointed into the sky now dark. "He is now a star of the night, one of the brightest in the sky, to be seen once a day for the rest of your life."

Nalon was absolutely astounded by the show of power which this wirinun held in the palm of his hands and felt quite sure that a gift had been imparted upon him from either Death or Evil.

"Enough of this," commanded Nalon, knowing now, within the blink of an eye that something must be done, for such power should not be possessed by one so cruel; and Goolay-yali, standing there unsure of himself, nursing his face as best he could, should not be permitted to roam the face of this new world as created by the Great Father Spirit. "I too shall wield errand and see justice done."

And with that said another blinding burst of light sprang from the depths of darkness and both Beereeun and Goolay-yali disappeared from view.

The gathered hunters were astounded by such power and sank to their knees and Bullai-bullai saw justice served to one so crawl. "Where are they?" she asked. "What have you done to them?"

"Just there," pointed Nalon with his lips. "At the rock; see."

Bullai-bullai looked and stared. The crawling menace of forever encroachment, called Beereeun, had been turned into an ugly lizard; and Goolay-yali, having whitish ash all over his face had been turned into similar: a pelican with coloured feathers to match his previous completion.

The hunters all around watched on completely astounded and the singing of the birds erupted once more, and the look upon each face changed to sheer happiness.

"Can you bring Weedah back?" asked Bullai-bullai.

"I cannot undo what has been done, but I can do something to ward off your misery by dispatching you from this life as a woman," said Nalon. "Look down and you shall see the wonders that begin to unfold, and the reason why these hunters now look upon you with smiles upon their faces."

And Bullai-bullai looked down and saw that she was dressed in many colours, being green, red and white, with a myriad of others to adorn her beauty. She then looked at Nalon and flapped her wings, launching herself into the night sky, the first parrot born to the world.

She had been transformed into the most beautiful of birds, even more beautiful than what Baiame had created.

THE SACRED TUKKERI

Many days had since passed.

Nalon was becoming tired when he fell down beside the Forbidden River and cupped some cool water into his palms, scooping it up into his mouth. The water fell from the sides where his lips failed to seal but he managed to gulp most of the water down.

"I am weary, Great Father," said Nalon into the air, "and you made good promise that I should not become weary of the journey set before me. What shall become of me, because I am so tired?"

Nalon staggered to his feet and struggled to get a foothold upon the level surface beside the river, and unhitched the Gayandi from its post at his waist band and turned it through the air to bring voice to it, to aid him in his desire.

Moments later and the Great Father spirit were standing there beside him. Before he could speak a single word Nalon gave way and fell to the ground exhausted.

"I need food," pleaded Nalon. "I cannot live on scraps alone, where no women can be found for which to give aid. Women are needed to gather the roots and berries, the nuts and yams."

"You are right," said the Great Father. "I have neglected you, and so from this day forth I shall grant you, and all men, a suitable reward in order to provide you with bursts of energy and strength."

The Great Father stalked over to the river and plunged his hand into it withdrawing a fish from within. He flung it over to the side of Nalon and the fish flapped about upon the ground as is drew air into its lungs and died.

"Eat this fish and you shall be nourished," said the Great Father. "It is called a tukkeri fish and from this day forth shall be sacred to men: it is not to pass the lips of women."

"Ah, thank you, Baiame; thank you," blurted Nalon in his delirious state. "I shall eat this tukkeri and regain my strength and recommence my quest on the morrow."

Yowie stood before Marmoo and did not look pleased at all.

"You must do something about this, Marmoo," said Yowie, though not very convincing with the way in which he spoke his words. "I am busily invested in creating monsters for which to eat the fodder of the land."

"Why must I do this thing for you; this something?" complained Marmoo quite realistically. "Did I not create the insects of the world to—?"

"Nothing..." shouted Yowie as he paced the ground before Marmoo, in front of the cave which was the home of Evil. "Everything you have done has been undone. All you have achieved has been thwarted."

"Am I to blame for that?" asked Marmoo. He then looked blankly at the fire before him and looked up again. "I tell you what I shall do. I shall cast before Nalon a surprise that will not be avoided."

"Ah, this sounds good," said Yowie. "What is it exactly you intend to do?"

"Deceive him, through and through, like no other has been deceived before him. I shall cast my magic and transform two women from thin air, and place them within the trunk of a tree. When Nalon comes past they shall tempt him, and being man he will falter."

Nalon was making reasonable progress upon his walkabout when two voices suddenly fell upon his ears; two subtle voices from some place quite near.

"Help us; help us please," said the voices.

"Where... where are you?" asked Nalon, mystified by the sweet sounds. So long it was since he had last heard a voice so sweet.

"Here," said one. "Over here, in the trunk of this tree."

Nalon stepped over towards it and looked it up and down. He recalled seeing the dark shadow near the gum tree of the Forbidden River and immediately thought it a trick to lure him. He staggered back several paces thinking this might be the same.

"You are a figment of my imagination," insisted Nalon. "You are not really there. What I hear is in my head."

"No," cried a voice once more. "We are here and can only to cast out with the true magic of goodness; from your cleansed soul can we be awarded freedom from our dilemma."

"But why were you put in the tree to start with; are you evil? Did you do something wrong? Are you being punished? Furthermore, how do you know of me and my inner spirit and power?"

"Thrice, no," came the reply. "And furthermore... we can sense the goodness within you. We have been mistreated by a former chief and wish now to walk the earth once more. Will you not give aid?"

Nalon considered it for a moment and decided that no real harm could come of this.

"I shall do my best," insisted Nalon. "Wait and I shall cast a wish upon the very cause of your frustration, and release you of your bonds."

And without further ado there stood two women before him who immediately fell to their knees and prostrated themselves before him.

"Stand up, please, and give introduction," insisted Nalon, feeling ashamed that he should willingly accept the grovelling of two women obviously cast from their clan. "I am Nalon."

"We are Kari [smoke] and Kala [fire]," said Kari.

"We are twins," added Kala. "And thank you from the bottom of our hearts.

And yes they were; twins like none other, very beautiful and young, fresh from the tree like fruit from a branch.

"Who has done this thing to you?"

"We don't recall," said Kari.

"So strange it is," added Kala.

"It is as though our clan has discarded us from their camp like our memories have been erased from our minds."

"But we are sure to have done nothing wrong," said Kari. "Please; allow us to serve you, our new master. We can fetch you food."

"Good berries and nuts," said Kala.

"I can serve you both in return," said Nalon with a smile, "by seeing to it that you are provided a clan to call your own."

"We will be happy to remain with you," said Kala, "always."

"Very well then," agreed Nalon with a smile, not wishing to upset the two. "It is getting late and it is time to make camp for the night. You shall gather some berries and nuts, and re-join me for a relaxing evening before a fire, one that I shall attend to and spark into life."

"Oh, thank you, Nalon; thank you so much," said the twins in unison, smiles formed upon their faces.

Nalon was transfixed.

As the sun commenced to fall below the horizon the fire began to die, only small flames showing themselves to the world. Nalon and the twins had eaten well and all moved away to shelter beneath a shelter made from bark, something the women had put together in very little time.

All were extremely satisfied within and Nalon felt that he had done a good turn by offering his aid as he did, helping the two from the captivity of the trunk. But now it was time for sleep and as Nalon placed himself within the shelter the two women placed themselves either side of Nalon: very close indeed.

Nalon felt a surge of panic but the two women felt this and combat it quickly, replacing his feelings of dread with feelings of comfort.

"The fire was warm," said Kala, "But the heat of the body is more appealing."

"More natural," added Kari.

"A good man should have many wives to help him stay warm at night," said Kala.

"Do you have a wife or concubine?" asked Kari.

"No," said Nalon. "I have no companion," was all the answer they received.

"We find you kind," said Kala.

"Yes we do," concurred Kari.

"And wish to remain with you as wives, to help you in your endeavours, from one day to the next." And with those words spoken they snuggled up even closer against the naked flesh of Nalon and all fell asleep."

The following morning Nalon had woken and standing beside the Forbidden River with a spear in his hand. Both Kala and Kari awoke and saw Nalon trying to spear fish. They soon fell in beside him.

"You should not work yourself too hard with hunting," said Kala.

"Hunting is a task for a man," reminded Nalon. "A woman gathers."

"We can do that," said Kari with an idea formed within her mind. "We can make a basket and place bait in it, and place this in the water, gathering together whatever will come. It will not be the same as hunting with a Spear."

"Yes," agreed Nalon. "That is true; it would be gathering. Very well, make your basket and place it through the water, gather whatever you can, but..."

"But what?" asked Kari, with a smile upon her sweet face.

Nalon was feeling as though he were losing his way. "If you catch a tukkeri then you must not eat it."

"We know this," said Kala. "That is something that could never be forgotten, for it is the law of the Great Father Spirit whom we call Napelle."

"Yes, he has many names," agreed Nalon. "But all are the same. A law is a law, and should never be broken." And seeing that the twins had accepted the task and law he quickly moved off further upriver to continue with his spear-fishing.

Kala and Kari moved up with a treacherous look upon their faces and made a basket from reeds and vines, and no sooner had they put this in the waters of the Forbidden River and they had caught themselves three tukkeri.

Kari looked up river and could see that Nalon was nowhere near. "Let us take these tukkeri to the rekindled fire and cook them: eat them for ourselves."

"I agree," said Kala. "We deserve to try the flesh of something that is sacred."

The tukkeri had cooked perfectly and both Kala and Kari ate the three tukkeri with great ease and satisfaction.

"It is no wonder the tukkeri is sacred and old men only," said Kala. "It is wonderful."

"I have never tasted anything so good," agreed Kari. "Why should men be the only ones to eat such good food? From this day on I shall eat as much tukkeri as I possibly can."

Suddenly, from out of nowhere, a voice thundered through the forest. "What is that I smell?" yelled Nalon from near the edge of the Forbidden River. "Do I smell tukkeri being cooked?" and the smell was unmistakable.

"Quickly, sister," gasped Kala urgently. "Let us be on our way. We have been caught and cannot surrender to punishment."

"You are right, he is too powerful," agreed Kari and they both got up and ran away.

Nalon came upon the camp and could clearly see that tukkeri had been eaten, the remains a true indicator: and the twins were gone.

Nalon fell upon his haunches at the edge of the fire and wept. He had faltered upon his task; he had been tempted by women to forgo his journey, strong contemplation on forever giving up on the walkabout so important.

Nalon looked up towards sky-world. "I am sorry, Great Father. I have let you down. I am weak and did give myself to the misgivings of companionship."

All day long he remained there, fretting over what he had done, cursing himself for his weakness, for his lack of courage in seeing his task completed. And he swore to himself that he would never again succumb to the power of women.

THE ENCOUNTER WITH THE WOMBAT

Yowie sat opposite Marmoo and congratulated him.

"Well done, my friend," said Yowie. "You have done what I could not. You have destroyed him."

"Not quite," replied Marmoo. "I can see into his mind and it speaks a different language to the rest of his body. He has faltered on his way, he has brought discredit to that stinking, Baiame, but he will be forgiven; I warn you now."

"Then you must go to him," voiced Yowie. "You must go to Nalon and destroy him whilst he is weak of flesh and not thinking clearly. You must go there now, to the fireplace, and destroy him, once and for all."

Marmoo was a little displeased with Yowie, for he appeared to be giving an order. "Why should I go? You go and kill him. You go and do as you will with him."

"I cannot kill him," said Yowie. "I am the Spirit of Death; I do not have the power to kill a living thing, only take what is mine when the last breathe is drawn. I can manipulate and direct, but I do not have the power invested in me to interfere with the strong and healthy. I can command a weak branch within a tree to fall haplessly upon the weak, but not with one so strong with the magic of Baiame behind him. You are the evil one; you are the Spirit of Evil; so cast yourself upon the earth in semblance of another and kill him for me."

"I tire of your needs, desires, treachery and lies," said Marmoo as he sighed. "If I do this then it will be the last."

"You shall be safe," urged Yowie. "Baiame will be powerless against you, but he will avenge me in some way, I know it; but I shall be ready with further creations of abnormal proportion."

"Very well," agreed Marmoo. "I shall go now and do with Nalon as you require, but this will be the last time you call upon me for service. I grow so very tired of it all."

"I promise," said Yowie.

The Spirit of Evil cast himself upon the earth not very far from where Nalon was camped. It was late in the day and the sun had gone to bed, the last bands of reds and oranges drawing to a close. Marmoo could see the sparks of the fire that Nalon had built, the sparks spitting into the air around it.

Marmoo went to step off towards Nalon and faltered for a moment.

At the fire, Nalon was looking beaten. A voice suddenly came to his ear; it was the voice of Baiame.

"Be warned," said Baiame. "Danger approaches."

Nalon looked up and then turned his head to look behind. He could see nothing.

Marmoo couldn't quite see Nalon, but the fire was well alight. As he stepped ever closer the figure of Baiame came before him.

"Ah, Baiame," said Marmoo, slightly startled. "I was expecting you, and then again thought you might be too late. You know you are powerless to destroy me."

"But I am not powerless to change your form," said Baiame with a smile and cast his magic to fall upon the Spirit of Evil. "I shall not interfere with the walkabout that Nalon is undertaking, and I shall not make it easy for you to disrupt it."

With that said Marmoo was changed into a wombat.

"And as a wombat you shall walk the earth for the remainder of your days," said Baiame.

"Never mind," said Marmoo. "I have already destroyed the ambitions of Nalon; his quest is over."

"You, yourself, know this to be untrue."

"He has lost his way, lost it when he took the company of Kari and Kala."

"So that is their names," said Baiame. "They shall be dealt with, in due course."

"You have not defeated me, Baiame," said Marmoo. "I still have life in me."

"But the danger you were to impose upon Nalon has now passed and I shall return to sky-world before my presence here rewards Yowie with more opportunity to create upheaval."

With those final words spoken, Baiame disappeared.

Marmoo could not see himself but could clearly feel the tightness of his skin, the itchy feel of the fur, and smell the stench of wombat in his nose. He was quite disgusted in himself.

Marmoo saw no way out but one and put it to the test. He scurried along, sure to be heard by Nalon, and drew closer to the camp fire.

Nalon finally came to view of Marmoo and Nalon looked up. He could see the wombat not far away in the dying light as night finally fell upon him and his surrounds. The wombat was coming straight for him.

Was this the danger that Baiame was trying to warn him about.

Nalon reached for one of his two spears and flung it with his entire mite towards the approaching wombat. The spear entered just below the neck and blood spurted from the wound, and the spear continued through the flesh and into the trunk of a tree. The wombat had been hit solidly in the thickness of his neck and had been stopped dead in its tracks.

Nalon wasted no time at all in dragging the wombat over to his dying fire and turned to throw more wood upon the coals along with a little tinder to aid the flames back to full life.

As he did this he remembered his spear and stood up to get it. What he saw struck him with great horror.

From the tip of the spear within the trunk of the tree, to the place where it had first struck the wombat, the blood was stirring. The blood was moving, swirling around as though alive. The blood was coming together, congealing, and forming a shape upon the ground. Nalon saw before him the shape of a man coming together upon the forest floor and the more he looked the more he was astounded.

Within the time it takes to snap a large branch the transformation of the body was complete. It stood up and pulled the spear from the tree and held it in his hand.

"Who are you?" asked Nalon. "Have you been sent here to aid me in my quest, to help me find Kala and Keri who have done wrong by me and the laws of the land, to help me find my way?"

"I am the Spirit of Evil, and you have set me free," said Marmoo. "Baiame had imprisoned me within the form of a wombat and you broke the flesh, and now I am free to roam the world as a man."

"Not with my spear," said Nalon, defiantly. "You shall give the spear back."

"If that is what you want then that is what you will get," said Marmoo with a wicked smile upon his face as he drew back the spear and prepared to throw it. He unleashed the power of his throw and the spear struck Nalon in the thigh, but Nalon being invested with great fury and hatred for Marmoo and the two women did pull the spear from his flesh wound and hurled it back at the body of Marmoo. It struck him in the heart and Marmoo fell to the ground, mouth agape in horror. The body slumped and lay there unmoving.

Nalon watched helplessly and placed his hand upon his wound which healed beneath the magic of his touch, a gift from Baiame, a wordless message of consent for him to continue with the walkabout.

The body of Marmoo suddenly came to life once more; beetles, grubs, spiders, ants, and many other forms of insect scurrying from the wound within the heart before feverishly devouring the flesh of the body. Marmoo had turned into his host and the host was destroying its maker. Marmoo was eaten away until nothing remained, not a bone left to rot into the ground. Once done with the feast, the insects of the world disappeared into the forest, to all corners of the night which had fallen upon Nalon.

Nalon sat there and contemplated what had happened. His hope had been rekindled. His task had been reset. He would start out in the morning and not stop until his walkabout was complete, and if he should fall upon Kala and Kari he would dish out the appropriate punishment as he saw fit.

THE KURRIA

Nalon was happy to leave the Forbidden River far behind him as he commenced to move towards where the sun said its goodnight. This direction he now called the west, and behind was the east; both north and south he was familiar.

He had been travelling for quite some time when he fell upon a small clan of some ten individuals, two of the young girls born to a man by the name of Pikuwa. It was Pikuwa that Nalon encountered first as he was carrying back to his fire a small kangaroo rat.

After brief introduction Nalon was eager to find out what entertained Pikuwa to eat as he did.

"You know it is against the law of the land to eat the meat of an animal, so created by the Great Father Spirit, which was created for the enjoyment of all?"

"I am, Nalon of Alkira," said Pikuwa. "But food is made scarcer than ever. There are more and more monsters the further we move from the Forbidden River. They are monstrous animals that eat everything in their path; not to mention the insects of this land which devour all."

"But you have birds to eat the insects," reminded Nalon.

"But the monsters," said Pikuwa. "To go without meat means to go without food. It is said that the Spirit of Death had something to do with it all, that he created wild beasts to rid the land of us."

"But you have spear and brain, brawn and cunning," said Nalon.

"This is true, but our numbers are so few," said Pikuwa. "But I shall put this right."

"How will you put this thing to mend?" asked Nalon.

"I have two daughters," said Pikuwa, "and both are just old enough to rear children. I shall see to it personally that they grow with child at my hearth in the very near future. The land will then always have us walking upon it."

"It is good that you think for your people," said Nalon. "It is good that you can provide for you wife, your children, and your clan."

And Nalon followed Pikuwa into the camp and all were introduced.

It was not long before Nalon stumbled upon concern. The Wawalag clan was ten strong. There were three men and three women; each wed to make for three couples. Pikuwa was the only member to yet have reared children and both of these were close enough to age for bringing children of their own into the world created by Baiame. Pikuwa had a wife but he now found her undesirable. Where were the husbands to come from for his children?

After all had retired and there was but Pikuwa and Nalon left at the fire, Nalon decided to question him on peculiarities, laws, and customs.

"Pikuwa," said Nalon. "How many clans are there nearby with men old enough to be husbands to your children?"

"Why, none, of course," said Pikuwa as a matter of fact. "The closest I know of is two days from here. The resources of the land does not allow for so many to be harboured so near. But without children to help us in old age, where would we all be. You yourself look to be growing in years."

"I am, but I feel much younger than I look," said Nalon.

"Well, I would like to offer you my children but I am unwilling to do this thing for you," said Pikuwa, rather bluntly.

"I would not accept anyway," said Nalon. "I am a wirinum on walkabout, to offer reminders to clans of the laws provided this land. I should honestly be speaking with you in regards to eating meat."

"Ah, but I have already offered my reasons and see no point in changing our ways. Unless you can see a way around this dilemma then my mind is made up."

"Did you know that the Great Father Spirit has given approval for men to eat the tukkeri," said Nalon.

"And of women?" asked Pikuwa.

"No, women must not eat the tukkeri; this is for men only."

"My clan will not get far with only men, and men there will only be after the women have all shrivelled away and died."

"It is a dilemma," said Nalon. "And where do you propose to find the men to wed your beautiful daughters."

"Wed," said Pikuwa, almost choking. "I cannot wed them."

"No, not you," said Nalon, thinking that Pikuwa had misheard him, "but the men to be their husbands; those men to help bring children to your hearth?"

"I shall do it," said Pikuwa proudly. "I shall give them the gift of my love and cherish the children they bring into this world. I shall be the father of those brought into this clan. I have already taken liberty with one of the other wives."

Pikuwa could see the disgusted look upon the face of Nalon.

"I am the wirinum of this clan and I alone shall see to it that duty is performed. The others are too worried about rearing children where food is so scarce, but I beg to differ with them all."

"You mean to say that you, the father, will have sexual pleasure with your daughters?"

"I shall, and do, and if this is not to your liking, Nalon, then maybe you should depart on the morrow for a clan more fitting to your desires."

Nalon stood up. "Maybe you are right. Maybe I shall leave on the morrow."

That night, but early in the morning just prior to first light as Nalon slept, a noise fell upon his ear. He quietly moved away from his shelter and positioned himself closer to the unsuspecting two. He could hear the two sisters talking about their father and the horrible way in which he took pleasures with them.

"Do you think it will work, Amarina [rain]?" asked Binda [deep water].

"Yes, I am sure," replied Amarina.

The two commenced to move away from the camp, and towards where there existed a huge depression in the area which had flooded with water. Nalon followed silently so as not to draw attention to his ever presence.

"There is a banyan tree there, near the water," said Amarina. "It is strong and reliable. There is a very strong strip of bark hanging from it. If we hide in the tree when our father comes to meet us he will be tempted to climb after us when we refuse to come down. I shall then cut the bark with the shell I have stolen: so that it will be loose."

"Maybe our father will miss the shell he uses to cut with and suspect something," suggested Binda.

"No, it is not a prized possession, so stop worrying," urged Amarina.

They were soon at the spot where the banyan tree grew.

"This is it," pointed Amarina. "You can see the stripped bark hanging there."

"Yes, I can," admitted Binda. "Come, let us climb the tree and await our father. Do you think he will be long?"

"No," said Amarina. "The sun comes now so he will be along this way shortly, looking for us in earnest."

Nalon placed himself behind another banyan nearby and decided to watch from a distance. He had full intention of coming out of hiding should the father prove to be acting in an inappropriate manner.

He had not been waiting long when their mother appeared.

"Binda; Amarina; where are you both?" called Willa [a wife].

The girls could see their mother calling and showed themselves.

"Up here mother," said Binda. "Hiding from father. He is after us, to pleasure himself upon us in ways that he pleasures himself with you and other women of the clan."

"This cannot be true, children," said the mother.

"Then come and see for yourself," offered Amarina. "Climb up here with us and watch, but be careful, for the bark is loose. Father will be along soon, as is his usual custom."

The mother climbed the tree and hid behind them so that Pikuwa could not see her when he approached.

Not much longer into the birth of the new day and Pikuwa came upon the banyan tree and looked around for the two he knew were supposed to be waiting nearby for him to attend.

"Binda; Amarina;" called their father. "Where are you? Come out now."

"We are up here, father," called Binda as both girls showed themselves up there in the branches. "We are here to keep you away. You have violated out bodies by taking liberties upon us, robbing us of our pleasures by having pleasures of your own. We will not allow this thing to happen any longer."

"You will do as I tell you both," ordered Pikuwa. "I shall do what I wish to do with the children of my hearth, even if that is to take pleasures as I have always done."

And he started to climb the banyan in great anxiousness to get hold of his children to beat them.

Pikuwa was half way up when suddenly the wife appeared, showing her head between the shoulders of the two girls.

"I do not believe what I hear and see, Pikuwa," said Willa. "But it shall happen no more." And with that said she, herself, applied the final cut to the bark and Pikuwa fell to the ground, flat upon his back, the bones in his legs and arms breaking.

He screamed out in pain as the two girls and mother descended from the tree.

"It is justice that you fall and meet your fate," said Willa. "You will stay here now and die a deserved death, for I should have known better when first the presumption of your behaviour entered my mind. Come, Binda; Amarina. He is your father no more."

And all three departed, leaving Pikuwa upon the ground, crying out in pain.

Nalon came out of hiding and looked upon the broken man.

"You should look at yourself, Pikuwa," said Nalon. "With your arms and legs broken as they are you could never again live on this land."

"Then I shall live in the water," said Pikuwa. "It is not far. If I cannot ever again move as a man can, going hunting, cooking food, walking, running, and swinging my arms with ease, then I shall allow the water to sustain and support my bulk from this day forth."

Yes," said Nalon. "You shall live in the water as vile as you are, for you deserve no essence of forgiveness. And from this day forth you shall be known as a kurria [crocodile]."

Nalon turned his back on Pikuwa who was transformed in appearance, and with arms and legs broken he crawled along on his big flat belly towards the water and swam away to find his home amongst the sunken logs and hollows of the nearby expanse of water.

Nalon watched as Pikuwa made his way to the water and considered all that had happened. Pikuwa did not deserve to live as a free man, able to hunt and run and leap about; he did not deserve to enjoy the rudiments of life; but he did deserve to suffer for all he had done to others, he deserved to suffer a long life in exile as a kurria. And so Nalon, seeing to ensure that Pikuwa lived a long and miserable life cast the magic bestowed upon him by Baiame, and said: "One more thing, Pikuwa. I shall provide you with a basic means for survival."

Nalon looked up into the sky and hundreds of birds could be seen moving high above the surface of the water, and with several words cast from his mouth dozens of them fell from the sky in flight and entered the water, turning into fish as they did so.

"You will now have something to eat, but you will always be a prisoner of this landlocked water source."

THE RAINBOW SNAKE

The Spirit of Death looked on from afar and saw the misery which was to become the life for Pikuwa, and felt as though he deserved to propagate and become a menace upon the land. And there before his eyes, Pikuwa saw a female kurria appear, lush with life and ready to mate, having been cast from the dusty ground. Yowie had taken from the creation of Nalon, and formed another: a female. Yowie had more power now due to past incursions of Baiame upon the land, but his newfound power was limited.

"And so that the young will be reared to live long and fruitful lives I shall enable you to travel far by providing access to and fro, by creating a flesh-eating monster called wonambi; and he shall do my bidding.

And having spoken those words, Yowie moved away in order for the wonambi to do as he was required.

A wonambi he was, Wonambi was his name, a monster of a snake, a python of humungous size, a constrictor of life, and four people in length and as thick in body: if not more. He was gold in colour with black markings and had a diamond-shaped head; with a huge appetite to match.

Wonambi moved across the dry ground in search for food, hungry as hungry can be, his tongue flicking out and tasting the air for scent of life.

When the sense of life fell over him it flourished through all his pours and all his senses. He had arrived upon the outskirts of the Wawalag clan. He knew there were two young females and five elder specimens who were available for him to savour and snack upon.

He continued on until upon them.

Wonambi curled himself around the camp and in great astonishment grew in size, so monstrous that he was now larger than life itself. The men and women of the clan woke from slumber, ran around and screamed, voiced of the horror before their eyes, and one by one Wonambi snatched them up and swallowed them whole.

Yowie smiled at the performance from his vantage point and was happy at what had happened, but now it was time for Wonambi to do further bidding, for Yowie could not change the landscape of the land, only create beasts of burden to help him fulfil his dream.

The sense of suggestion within Wonambi was so strong that he made immediately for the water where Pikuwa had been imprisoned, and from the northern most edge, and the clan of men and women in his stomach bulging here and there, he used his body to carve great rivers and channels upon the land, so far afield that the coast was reached within a matter of a single day.

Wonambi was worn out from his task and fell into a deep slumber and during the exile from consciousness his body reformed and shrunk back to its original size: but he was to become a menace to all the men and women of the land, for many thousands of years to come.

Pikuwa looked up from the surface of the water, his smile evident for all time to come, a grin of malice frozen upon his lips. He had been provided a good home, with good food; had a wife, and was called father: all he wanted in life provided him. He was free, could roam here and there, to go wherever it pleased him, and he would populate the land and have his way with the men and women of his world by condemning them to death, to gnaw upon their flesh whenever he received the opportunity.

Pikuwa was happy. Wonambi was famished. Yowie was only just begun.

LIFE AFTER DEATH

Mopoke was the wirinum of the Bird clan, the wisest man, so it is said, to be known to walk the earth. He was the youngest of the clan and looked up to by young and old – to the youngest of young he was adored. It was extremely strange for one as young as Mopoke to be in position as wirinum, but he had proved his abilities beyond expectation. Mopoke only had a single flaw, and that was his inability to voice his opinion in the face of the wrongful doings of Eagle-hawk.

Eagle-hawk was the chief of Bird clan. He had currently organised a great hunt where every available hunter of the clan went off in search for food: what they came back with was little more than a few kangaroo rats.

The fires were started and a corroboree was to be begun, but lengthy discussion would be the discourse in order to consider the future of the clan.

Eagle-hawk was standing there on the edge of the clearing, where the cooroboree was to take place when he heard a noise from behind. He turned quickly to see Nalon standing there.

"Who are you to be creeping upon me?" questioned Eagle-hawk.

"Forgive me," said Nalon. "My name is Nalon and I am the chief of the Alkira clan."

"Ah, I have heard of you," said Eagle-hawk. "Yes indeed, for it is you that gave the world the cooroboree which are to perform."

Mopoke also saw Nalon and moved in beside the chief of Bird.

"I am Mopoke," said Mopoke. "So you are Nalon, chief of the Alkira. We have heard of you." Both Nalon and Mopoke exchanged a knowing look, as though Nalon knew the secret past that Mopoke had lead, and Mopoke knew of Nalon and his cooperation with Baiame.

"And may I ask, what is it you hear?" queried Nalon.

"That you are travelling the land," interrupted Eagle-hawk, "and trying to put-things-right. But I tell you now, there is nothing the matter."

Nalon could see the preparations taking place near the centre of the camp. "You are preparing meat for eating. Only the meat of animals so created by the Spirit of Death, Yowie, is permitted."

"We are dying, Nalon," said Eagle-hawk. "What am I to do? There is no life after death. No one here wants to die and so we shall eat whatever we are able to gather and hunt."

Nalon looked at Eagle-hawk, seemingly puzzled. "What do you mean no life after death; of course there is life. Your spirit within departs your body and reforms in another. You might come back as a kangaroo rat or a lyrebird."

"No," said Eagle-hawk, "there is no life after death, and I can prove it."

A man named Crow had joined the circle of discussion and watched in all eagerness as Eagle-hawk set about to prove that there was no life after death. He bent down and picked up a pebble from the ground. "Please, follow me and you shall see."

They all followed Eagle-hawk: Nalon, Mopoke and Crow. Down to the river they walked and then stood beside it. Eagle-hawk threw the pebble out into the middle of the river and it disappeared from view.

"Just like death, the spirit within ceases to exist, just like the pebble no longer exists."

"It still exists," argued Crow, seemingly out of place amongst the four. "It is no longer a pebble of the land but now a pebble of the river. Just because you can no longer see it does not mean that it does not exist."

72

"No, you are wrong," said Eagle-hawk. "You, Crow, exist. When you are dead your body doesn't take another form, you just simply disappear from existence; I would not see your spirit find another body nor home."

"But even now you cannot see my spirit, even when I am alive."

"The spirit within cannot be killed like the body," said Nalon, "just like the pebble still exists in the water: it as simply changed within the element of its existence."

"A pebble is a pebble," said Mopoke as a challenge, but both he and Nalon knew the truth of the situation: Mopoke simply wished for Eagle-hawk to be convinced, "and a very poor example of what it is we seek."

"What we seek is an answer," said Eagle-hawk, "that life after death, either, does or does not exist. Since you cannot prove it does exist I must therefore be sure that there is no life after death, and therefore the spirit is left, not only without a home, but also without the elements in which to continue any form of existence." Eagle-hawk looked at each and every one of those standing around. "Is there anyone here that can prove otherwise," and looked to Nalon.

"A caterpillar," said Nalon. "It dies but is reborn as a butterfly. The spirit has moved from one to the other. We know the spirit of the caterpillar cannot be lost for it is trapped within the cacoon."

"Yes," agreed Crow. "The body has changed from one form to another; one existence to another. The spirit of the caterpillar has definitely moved from one to the other. The cocoon is simply a measure of security that is performed to ensure that no other spirit takes the element of the butterfly."

"This is why we come back in other forms," added Mopoke, feeling as though his secret would break soon and that all would know of his past. "We have no measure to ensure the safe transition of the spirit from one body to another, so it is reasonable to expect that our spirit could come back as a kangaroo rat."

"But we eat kangaroo-rats," said Eagle-hawk. "We could be eating out ancestors."

"Baiame made the law of no meat-eating for a reason, Eagle-hawk," said Nalon. "The laws should not be broken, but elements of the law can be changed where the need is born in the same way that our spirit finds a new body when it is needed. The basic fundamentals of existence remain in the same way that the roots of the law still remain. The current law allows for tukkeri to be eaten by men alone, but both men and women can enjoy the meat of the wild beast created by Yowie, these being monstrous in size. Yowie did not make the beasts to be easily killed by hunters. They are strong and resilient. They will eat all the green of the earth if they could, just to see you and your clan die of hunger, but you shall still come back as another. But seek not an early death, for the life you lead is momentous and should be cherished for what it is."

"And what is it?" asked Crow.

"It is the opportunity of a lifetime," said the intelligent Mopoke, "to show Baiame that we are sanctioned by his laws, that we are happy to abide by his laws, and that we are thankful to him for allowing us to experience this existence. Some of us will receive a second chance soon after death, but not many: some will have to wait." Again, Mopoke and Nalon shared that knowing look.

"Eagle-hawk," said Nalon. "I see that my time here is not required. I see in your eyes the understanding of the laws. The Bird clan is a good clan and understands well the laws of the land. Heed the laws of Baiame, always."

"Thank you, Nalon," said Eagle-hawk. "Although your time with us has been short, it has been extremely valuable and educational."

With that said Nalon parted ways with Eagle-hawk, Mopoke and Crow, and made his way further inland, away from the Forbidden River and towards the land of the wild beasts.

Nalon hadn't gone more than a few paces when Mopoke stepped up beside him. Nalon turned as Mopoke spoke to the others: "Eagle-hawk; Crow; I shall be alone shortly, but first I must speak with Nalon."

Eagle-hawk waved consent and disappeared with Crow.

And now they were alone.

"I saw the way in which you looked at me, Nalon," said Mopoke. "I must tell you, however, that I have changed my ways for the better."

"I can see this," said Nalon. "You know there is more to me than meets the eye. I know who you used to be and what you have done, but the experience has made you a better man. I know all about your past life as Murkupang."

MURKUPANG

The enormous giant-of-a-man looked down upon his mother-in-law as she looked up from her weakened form.

"You have not brought me anything to eat," said Gurley [a native willow].

"There is nothing, old woman," said Murkupang briskly and with venom. "I barely find enough these days to feed myself, let alone you, too."

"I am the mother of you wife. You must tend to me."

Murkupang could take no more. He would spend all his day in search of food and still not find enough to appease his own hunger. With a dead wife on one hand and an old mother-in-law on the other, where was he to get the roots, berries, and seeds to help keep himself satisfied?

"I have had enough and will leave this clan," said Murkupang hastily. "Never again shall I feed you, whether my responsibility or not. There is simply not enough in these parts to feed us all."

And so Murkupang departed the vicinity of the clan immediately and found himself a nice little cave on the slope of a mountain side which overlooked a stream of clean water. Game appeared to be bountiful in this new area and the best thing of all was that there were no other people around.

Murkupang spent the next few days setting up his cave and hunting. He gathered wood for his fire, and food for his stomach, mostly that which was against the laws as set by Baiame.

Gurley, however, knew she would not live long without the help of a hunter as good as Murkupang to bring food to her: what was it to her that he went hungry; was he not young enough to take care of himself? Was he not a real man?

So she set off in search of her son-in-law with two trackers beside her. These two men would stay by her and help ensure that Murkupang carried out his duties as a good hunter and relation should.

It was not long before the three fell upon the cave that Murkupang called his own and as expected he was away attending to his hunger. The old woman looked down and saw his huge footprints in the dirt, but she also saw something else. There before her eyes were the tracks left by the dingo.

Gurley looked at the two young men. "Gather some wood, quickly, for Murkupang has dingoes with him. We shall build a fire just to the entrance of this cave and suppress your scent with the smell of smoke."

The two young men acknowledged her command and jumped into action gathering the wood required along with a handsome amount of kindling.

No sooner had they returned and the old woman started the fire before the cave entrance. "Come nearer and have this smoke descend upon you. May your scent be covered and smeared, hidden from the very noses of the animals he now has in his care, for the dingo is of the Madhi clan, and they are not a pleasant people: even when on two legs instead of four."

The two men spent some considerable time allowing the smoke to spoil them before the old woman drew them away from the fire and wrapped them up in the bark of the stringybark tree.

"You now have no lingering man-smell and look like trees," said Gurley, proudly. She then moved closer to the cave entrance though some distance from it and awaited the return of Murkupang.

Her wait was short for Murkupang soon returned with two dingoes at his heel and plenty of meat upon his strong and resilient shoulders, meat from a kyeema [kangaroo of the Dawn of Man: which has a short face, single huge claw on back foot, long front arms – a procoptodon goliath, almost twice as tall as a man].

Murkupang saw the mother-in-law as he approached and the two dingoes went to have a sniff. The dingoes knew her to be a friend for Murkupang threw half the meat down before her as he passed into his cave and said, rather venomously: "If you want this then take it, but I shall not cook it for you. When I wake on the morrow I would like to see you gone."

And then, quite suddenly, Murkupang stopped dead in his tracks and turned around. He looked Gurley in the face and saw a tiny smile there upon her. He looked down at his dingoes and ordered them into the vicinity, to check for unwanted characters, for Gurley could not be trusted.

After a thorough search and finding nothing, Murkupang was satisfied that the coast was clear and that the old woman was by herself. He moved into the coolness of the cave and cooked his own meal upon the fire within, the dingoes waiting for their share of the hunt for they had much aided in the bringing down of the kyeema: they were shortly joined by a further six dingoes.

As the sky drew darker, Gurley sprang into action. She brought the two young men nearer and handed them torches of which they would set alight. On achieving good flame upon their torches they set fire to the few shrubs near the entrance to the cave and some other sticks that they had deposited on their own accord as all those within the cave slept.

Murkupang awoke with a start and started to choke to death and the eight dingoes howled to the pain each and every one of them was suffering. The noise was so loud that Yowie was drawn to it.

The Spirit of Death looked down upon the scene of mayhem and saw that Murkupang and the eight dingoes were dying. This was now his opportunity to have his sinister thoughts brought into play, to see a small portion of his vengeance performed against Baiame.

He cast his magic and Murkupang was turned into a mopoke, and the eight dingoes into black jay, cockatoo, crow, quail, large spiders, hawk, magpie and mynah; but this was by sheer accident. Yowie had meant to create insects only but his power was dwindling: he would have to hope for Nalon to call upon Baiame once more, or for some other cause to fill his need and desire in order for his power to grow again.

The birds having descended further into the cave flew off into the night, and mopoke headed towards the Forbidden River to quench his dying first brought on by the smoke. Each had its own character and needs. Baiame had created dingoes through Nalon, but he, Yowie, had changed them further, showing how heinous he was, despite his magical error.

"And so," said Mopoke, "as I went about my business as a mopoke I was struck down by a larger bird of prey, hence my spirit escaping from the body of a bird and into the body of person."

Nalon looked him in the eye. "You have descended from evil and started the climb to greatness. You are very young but hold such a grand position amidst the clan you now call home. I should hope that you would give me aid from this day forth and see to it that the laws, as laid down by Baiame, are adhered to."

"I will do my best," said Mopoke. "But times are hard."

"You shall shape a Gayandi, like this one," said Nalon as he untied the Gayandi from his waist belt. He handed it to Mopoke to look at. "And use it to hear the magic words of Baiame; but be warned; use it sparingly, for where good is present the evil of Yowie shall follow."

"Thank you, Nalon," said Mopoke with a smile. "I shall see to it immediately."

Nalon was ready to depart company. "Good luck to you Mopoke and I hope that the clan in which you reside prospers."

No further word was necessary and Nalon turned to be on his way; Mopoke simply stood there and watched as he walked away.

BUBBUR

Nalon was sitting by his fire as he threw some fish upon the hot stones within, immediately the flesh seemed to come to life, spitting and hissing as it commenced to cook. He was relaxed and comfortable, happy within: the most happy and content he had been for a long time.

Baiame had promised him a harvest, each day if required, so that he would be able to more freely concentrate upon his task at hand instead of worrying over the sounds from his stomach. But a new sound found his ear today, before the dying light of day disappeared for slumber to take its place.

Nalon sat up erect and listened intently. He said nothing. And then the figure of a man, young and happy, a smile upon his face, appeared from the thickness of the jungle.

"Oh; I saw the light of the fire and thought... I thought you might be of my clan," said the young man.

Nalon stood up. "Please; welcome. Sit and be patient for I am about to serve food."

"A most welcome delight for I am famished," said the young man. "But I have plenty." And from upon his shoulder he threw down a small kyeema, but even one so young weighed almost as much as a man.

"Enough to feed an army of insects and a large clan," said Nalon. "But keep your meat till morning."

"It might not keep," said the young man.

Nalon leant forward, held his palm up towards the dead kyeema and closed his eyes, performing his magic. He opened them again. "It will keep; trust me," and sat down. "What is your name?"

He appeared stunned by what had just happened but answered the question most politely.

"I am Burnum [a great warrior]," said Burnum.

"A great name for one so young," said Nalon smiling, poking his large tukkeri with a stick.

"Some are named at ritual, others at birth," said Burnum. "I was so named at birth due to my size and my ancestors... and by the amount of pain I caused my mother at the time of her labour."

"A fitting name all the same. I am Nalon."

"I have heard of you," said Burnum. "A wirinum from Alkira, if I am not mistaken."

"You are not," said Nalon. "The fish is ready. Here, take this bark."

Nalon cut some fish away and placed it upon the bark for Burnum to eat and then placed some on his own. They ate in silence and when finished resumed the conversation.

"From what you tell me you cannot be very far from the borders of your clan," said Nalon.

"Not far at all," replied Burnum. "It is the Olono [a hill] clan. We overlook the vast land of plenty where monstrous beasts roam free and when we glance over our shoulder to the east we see the jungles, and sometimes, when early in the morning and the sun shines at its brightest, there we can see the Forbidden River."

"So I am close to the land of plains," said Nalon as a matter of fact.

"You are."

"Do you hunt the beasts that roam that land?"

"No," said Burnum. "They are too large and fearsome."

"But you are a great warrior," reminded Nalon. "And you carry a kyeema: that in itself is a monster of a beast."

"This is true."

"There is no law broken by eating neither fish nor the flesh of a beast created by the manipulations of the Spirit of Death."

"It is something we must remind ourselves of each day," said Burnum, as though it was an accomplishment so hard to achieve. "We do break the law so seldom but hunger strikes so often."

"You must gather your men and learn new ways," advised Nalon. "Find a way and harness your skills to bring down the creatures of Death."

"Maybe you are right," said Burnum. "But the first thing I must do is get this meat back to the clan. It is in offering to the mother and father of the girl to become my wife."

"Ah," said Nalon, "a bride price."

"Yes, Warrah [honeysuckle] is her name, the most beautiful of all the clans," said Burnum with a smile.

"Well, Burnum; stay here the night and rest, and I shall accompany you in the morning so that you may make your offering."

The following morning the two men made their way into the camp of the Olono clan and something seemed to be the matter. Everyone was so glum on the day of the big feast and celebration that it was as though the two men had stumbled into the wrong camp.

Burnum then saw his mother and father in-laws and moved over to them straight away with the kyeema stretched over his shoulder. Nalon followed at a reasonable distance behind him.

Burnum let the kyeema fall from his shoulders and onto the ground before making it clear that his part of the deal had been completed.

"My offering to you, mother and father, for the hand of the woman I love and with all my heart," said Burnum with happiness and sheer joy. "For the feast tonight there will not be an empty belly."

The mother-in-law looked up into the sparkling eyes of Burnum and spoke these words: "You are too late, Burnum. You have arrived just in time for her funeral."

"Funeral," said a stunned Burnum, for the words could not be true. "Funeral... what has happened; tell me?"

"Warrah went out three days ago, just after you left on your hunt," started the mother. "She wanted to collect some honey for the feast and went by herself, to reflect upon the journey of her childhood; to reflect on the happiness to come. But on her way she fell upon a nest of eggs of the wonambi, the largest of them all, the one we call Bubbur."

"Bubbur?" he was a little shocked. "You need not say any more," said Burnum. "You shall show me the body. I will go to the place of her death and bring her back to life with the aid of Nalon," and he looked towards the wirinum behind him. The mother and father to be also looked, and staring at Nalon was the entire clan.

"You cannot," said the mother. "Her entire body has been broken, not a single bone within her has been spared."

Burnum was silent for a moment and immediately he thought of the conversation with Nalon the night before.

"The wonambi is a monster creation of the Spirit of Death and as such it is our duty, in order to follow and obey the laws of Baiame, to see to it that death is delivered it. We must see to it that all creatures, so huge in number and size that walk the plains, marshes, jungles and forests, are dealt what they deserve." Burnum turned round on the spot to look everyone in the eye as he spoke. "We must learn new ways of hunting so that the beasts of Death are hunted down and destroyed for all time, and to start this quest we must destroy the wonambi that has destroyed my life."

"It cannot be done," said the mother.

"It can, and it will," said Burnum, and he walked away to contemplate the hunt.

Burnum had called the clan together; a week had passed. "All of you listen to me. You must give me your blessing by providing me with aid. Go now into the forest and bring back as much beefwood gum as you can."

"We already have beefwood gum," said a voice from the gathered, one of the thirty-strong clan of men, women, and children.

"I need it to be fresh," continued Burnum. "Help me in this quest. Gather what you can and be back here before the sun is at its highest. Bring the gum stuffed inside innards; it will be easier to carry."

My midday Burnum had gathered together eight strong men including himself: Nalon simply joined in the hunt to observe, not to give aid, for he was too old to fool around with hunting big game.

The hunters followed the lead of the one who had found Warrah, her mangled body almost too hard to recognize. Kalti [a spear] lead them directly to the place of her death.

"This is it," said Kalti to Burnum. "This is where I found her, and the eggs were just there." He pursed his lips in the direction.

All that was left were the eggshell remains of the young that had been born.

Burnum looked at the site and then looked up at the trees. "As I expected. The mother has made a good choice in picking this place to lay her eggs: plenty of sun and plenty of shade. These trees will give us the edge in battle."

"How?" asked Kalti. "What are we to do? We have nothing but these huge animal innards stuffed with gum. We have only a single spear each amongst us for you told us to bring only the gum; that gum was all we needed."

"Trust me now, Kalti and I promise you this; you will trust me always." Burnum turned to the others. "Strip the bark from these trees and lay a platform upon the lower branches. This will be the site from which to make our attack, but work as quietly as possible so as not to alert Bubbur as to our presence."

The eight men set to work and Nalon watched, and within a short span of time the trees soon had a platform each on which to sit or stand. They all climbed into the trees and onto the platforms, innards filled with gum at the ready.

"Now you can make as much noise as you possibly can and when Bubbur and her young appear you shall follow my lead," ordered Burnum.

The men bashed the tree trunks and platforms, sang out as much as their lungs would allow, and after a short period of time a noise fell upon their ears. They fell to silence and listened. Bubbur was close, but there was something else; there were all the young that had recently hatched, all very large and as thick as the leg of a man.

When Bubbur first appeared before them the men seemed horrified. Bubbur was thicker than the body of a man and a monstrous length; the longest snake any of them had ever seen.

"Keep up the noise," commanded Burnum.

The noise continued and Bubbur drew closer. When she was beneath the men she stretched out to try to reach them and as she opened her mouth and flicked out her tongue, Burnum dropped a lump of gum into the gaping mouth.

Bubbur drew her mammoth head back and seemed to chew upon the gum, opening and closing her mouth to be rid of the restriction.

"Quickly, all of you," urged Burnum. "Do as I have done, get gum into the mouths of all the young."

And it wasn't long before every single snake beneath them was without the use of their mouths. Suddenly, Burnum leapt like a hero from the platform and to the ground below with his spear in his hand and he killed Bubbur with just five thrusts of the weapon in his hand. His comrades followed his example and leapt down, too. In no time at all there were over a dozen lifeless forms before them: all the snakes had been killed, including Bubbur, the most feared wonambi of them all.

Burnum looked around at the others. "What we have done here today is a platform from which to deliver justice to other beasts created by the hand of Death. We shall no longer cry from hunger, for the flesh of those monsters that tarnish this land shall be our just reward."

Many screams of jubilation, congratulations, and agreement went up into the air and they commenced with their journey back to Olono, taking with them all they could of the purist meat – the young snakes – for Bubbur was too large and deserved nothing more than to be left as fodder for the insects of the world.

Burnum looked at Nalon. "Thank you, Nalon, for without your suggestion I would never have thought in the way I had. You have opened the door for us all and we hope to give honour to Baiame by following his laws."

"I am sure that you will live up to his standards," said Nalon.

"Come," said Burnum. "Come now and join us, help us celebrate."

"No, I cannot," said Nalon. "I must continue with my journey and see the laws grasped by the hearts of all the clans."

"Very well, I understand, but you shall not depart here without a gift," said Burnum.

"A gift," said Nalon. "What sort of gift would an old man like me require?"

"A simple gift," said Burnum. "Well; some might say it is more like an action." And Burnum did the strangest thing; he smiled and walked away.

Nalon looked at Kalti who was the only man left behind. "What do you think he means?" asked Nalon.

"I am your gift," said Kalti. "I shall help protect you wherever you shall go. I shall always be by your side. My eyes are closed to your magic, my heart open to your cause, and my flesh and bone honoured to respect your every command but one."

"And what single command is it that you will not obey?" asked Nalon.

"Why; stay here, of course; and any other command which means the same."

And with that spoken there was nothing further to add.

Nalon and Kalti were now brothers and continued with the walkabout.

THE GOANNA

Nalon and Kalti had fallen upon a clan whose camp was sited right on the verge of the great plain, where large beasts could be found roaming the land and devouring it of all its goodness.

The shelters of those within the camp were kept well back from the openness of the land which seemed to go on forever but it was easy to see through the gaps of the trees and branches: far easier to see out than it was to see in, for the clan remained well camouflaged where they were and the fires that they burnt all day and night helped to keep the beasts of the plains and nearby swamp lands at bay.

Nalon came to view first and the chief stood up and walked over to him.

"I am Yarran [an acacia tree], chief of the Leena [a possum] clan, although we have been known to be referred to as porcupine due to the amount of spears each man carries," said Yarran. "And who are you to trespass upon our land?"

"Trespass," queried Nalon. "Forgive me, but land cannot be possessed; there are no possessions other than a coolamon [plate (bowl) and digging tool], grinding stone, digging stick and spear; what else do you need?"

"It is not for you to question our way of life," said the chief. "Who are you to come amongst us and decide our fate?"

"I am Nalon."

Another man approached. "I am Woorak [from the plains] and the wirinum for the Leena. We have heard of you, Nalon."

"If I am to interpret all by the expression upon your faces then it would be an easy task to see that you do not consider my appearance as either a great opportunity, rewarding, or satisfactory."

"You hold yourself in high esteem; I should not have to explain myself to you, but shall," said Yarran. "We have left the Forbidden River far beyond and have founded a new way in which to live. Living on the flesh of animals is now our way of life."

"Eating the flesh of evil is not unlawful, but there are unlawful meals being eaten."

The chief looked around him. "How can you tell?"

"You call yourselves the Leena clan, and I know this to mean that you are pygmy-possum-eaters."

"There is no pretence here," said Woorak, endeavouring to save face. "We do not mean unwell towards you but there are others close by that cannot be trusted."

"The Tatya [goanna] clan," said Kalti.

"And how do you know that?" asked Woorak.

"I am from not-so-far-away," said Kalti and he pursed his lips towards the general direction of his clan.

"Then you know they are thieves," said the chief.

"They steal meat from you," started Kalti, "like you steal land from the creator."

Nalon smiled for he saw a victory in this and felt as though Kalti had already proved himself upon this journey of theirs.

"We were created to live upon this land," said the chief. "If we are not to take it to live upon then what is to be done with it?"

"You know as well as any other," said Nalon, "that a hunter gatherer is nomadic and that such possession is entirely unnecessary."

"You are right," said the chief, "but we do not need to walk about. We have all we need, right here."

"And you shall rape the land of all it has," said Kalti.

"And your need to walk about should not be for seeking food alone," added Nalon. "A walkabout is a spiritual awakening: a way of life."

"That is what walkabout is to you, not to us. To us it is simply walking about. As for raping the land; this is not true," said Yarran. "We have quartered the area. We take from one before moving onto another. Our clan is small and can reap the rewards by living in this way. But I fail to see why I should have to explain myself to you. I could have you taken away and skewered with a spear if I wanted."

"Let us not be hasty," interjected Woorak who seemed to have a worrying frown grow upon his naked forehead. "Nalon is a representative of all that is good and shall be forwarded great hospitality."

The chief considered within just a few beats of his heart. "You may stay and eat; shelter and enjoy our company," said Yarran, "but do not try and change our ways. Woorak will see to your comforts until you are ready to depart."

"Thank you," said Nalon. "But before we proceed please allow me one more thing. I am a representative of Baiame and as such have the power to lay commandments. From this day forth the meaning behind the term walkabout shall be revered: a spiritual awakening, a time to reflect upon the laws of the land."

Woorak answered before Yarran had the opportunity. "This I shall see to, Nalon. Our hunters shall carry those words upon their lips wherever they shall go."

Not very far away the Tatya clan were eating the last meal of the day and preparing for night when two men moved away from the fire for privacy; these were the chief and the wirinum. The chief of the clan was Derain [from the mountains] and the wirinum was Kami [a prickly lizard].

"Did you hear the report from the hunters?" asked Derain.

"Yes," replied Kami. "The Leena are planning another hunt for pygmy-possums."

"Yes indeed," said Derain. "I think we should make plans for interference. I grow tired of treading lightly, this time I would like to walk right in amongst them and fool them from the start."

"That will not be an easy task," said Kami. "They know we are thieves."

"We are not thieves," scolded Derain. "A thief only steals from those who have possessions, but Baiame is against this hoarding."

"I disagree," said Kami. "If they hunt and catch food then that is their possession."

"But their hunt is unlawful and so they must be punished," said Derain.

"You do not need to convince me," reminded Kami. "I am as good a thief as any other."

Derain turned with a smile. "Forgive me, Kami, for I was simply thinking out aloud. But the time has come for us to really deceive the Leena, once and for all."

"How do you consider doing this?" asked Kami.

"I shall tell you," said Derain, and he explained in full the plan he was hatching inside his head.

A lone hunter from the Tatya fell upon the Leena and appeared to be exhausted. He was immediately accosted and placed before the chief.

"What is the meaning of this?" questioned Yarran: Nalon, Kalti, and Woorak standing close by. "I am Yarran, chief of the clan."

"I am sorry. I am known as Ganan [from the west]," said the man. "I lost my way and was confronted by an enormous beast. I was chased and am so tired. I fall upon you for water in order for me to continue on my way."

"Where are you from?" asked Yarran.

"I am from the Tatya clan," replied Ganan, still pretending to be exhausted, living his lie, deceiving those before him.

"You are a thief," accused Yarran. "If I give you water then you will soon be asking for food."

"No," pleaded Ganan, "this is not true. We are like the herbivores of the great plain; none of the Tatya eats meat. It is disgusting to us. We love honey from the bee more than life itself."

Yarran appeared shocked and seeing the distaste upon the face of Ganan only made the story more truthful. "I did not know that," said Yarran. He turned to a hunter. "Bring this man some water, quickly."

"Thank you, Yarran," said Ganan. "Derain is my chief and he will be ever thankful for your generosity. If ever you need us he will be sure to give aid."

"We need no aid," said Yarran. "The most arduous task we undertake is when hunting pygmy-possum, which we will do on the morrow, but even in that we do not need help."

"I thank you anyway and shall advise my chief of your greatness, for we need aid even in gathering yams, roots, and berries, for the appetite of the Tatya is so strongly fixed to all essentials as brought forth by the land, in accordance with law."

"Laws are changing," lectured Yarran, "and always for the better."

The hunter from Tatya departed and Nalon turned silently to Kalti. "Do you see what I see?"

"I see a flood of lies," answered Kalti.

"So it would seem," agreed Nalon, "but I would be unjust to act so abruptly, to convict a man and his tribe before seeing for ourselves the deceit take shape."

Ganan stood before his chief.

"That is exactly what he said, Derain," said Ganan, "word for word."

"Good," said a satisfied Derain as he sat there with a large bone within his fist, chewing on the flesh falling from it. "If they are to hunt on the morrow then we shall make ourselves available." Derain looked at Ganan. "You have done well and have carried out your orders perfectly. The Leena now believes us to be like a common leaf-eater and know how just we are in returning good deeds done upon us. Thank you, Ganan."

"It has been a pleasure, Derain," said Ganan as he turned and moved away, stopping by the fire to steal a slice of meat from upon the bark of another. Derain simply sat and watched, none other seeing the theft.

"Did you see that, Kami?" asked Derain of his wirinum.

"No, Derain; what happened?"

"Ganan just stole a piece of meat from another, and not a sole saw him do it."

"Ah, well; I refuse to believe that you are without soul, Derain; and secondly I am so happy to see Ganan living up to the standards of our clan."

"Yes indeed. And now I want you to organise a gathering tonight so that I can give orders, and on the morrow we shall live up to our name as thieves and the Leena shall learn of our love for meat."

The way of the hunt was a simple affair as Nalon and Kalti were to experience, but it was sheer overkill: an oversight of the Leena which would be afforded much criticism by Nalon.

The hunters were organised in the shape of a half moon and when ordered were to make much noise. Such a racket would vibrate across the land that all pygmy-possums in the area would be forced from hiding and into a corridor within the trees. Along they would scamper until having reached an end, where they would be habitually forced to the ground, where traps had been laid.

All appeared ready when Yarran heard men approach from behind. He turned. The first one he saw was Ganan.

"I see you have returned," said Yarran as he looked beyond him. "And have brought the entire Tatya, or so it would seem. Are you all lost and looking for water?"

Ganan did not answer but the chief of Tatya did. "I am Derain, chief of the Tatya. I come in peace to thank you for what you have done and to provide help in your hunt. Ganan has told me all about you and I am happy to give aid."

"We need no aid," said Yarran. "My men are all ready and the hunt is about to commence."

"Tell me, Yarran," started Derain. "How long will the hunt take?"

"Much of the morning; why do you ask?"

"I am a learned man and chief, and know that the hunt will take, as you have stated, most of the morning," said Derain. "You then must gather the dead and skin the pygmy-possums before carrying them away to your camp. There will be cooking and the preparations for turning the skins into items of great trade. There is much work to be done and we can help you by providing one essential item to help keep you awake and full of life."

"What, and how, is that?" asked Derain.

"We shall gather honey in order for you to feed. Honey will also go well with your meat. We are good tree climbers and you are not, for us to help you in this way will please us all. We would prefer not to come near you when you eat your meat as it disgusts us all, but we will do what we can to repay you."

Yarran looked at Woorak and could see no reason to shun the offer.

"I shall hereby accept you offer," said Derain. "As for now we must commence whilst time is on our side. The pygmy-possums would only just have returned to their slumber, hence, when woken early will be all the more tired and disorientated."

"I understand," said Derain. "I shall see you again with coolamons overflowing with more honey than you and your clan has seen in a lifetime. I promise, we shall not interfere with you hunt."

"Thank you, Derain," said Yarran, and the hunt commenced.

It was well past noon when the sun was high, that the hunt and skinning had been completed. Nalon stood beside Yarran and looked unhappy.

"Do you see what you have created?" asked Nalon of the chief.

"I see nothing more than food-for-plenty," answered Yarran.

"You have over killed," indicated Nalon of all the corpses before him. "Every pygmy-possum in the area has been destroyed. There is more here than you can eat. Have you changed your mind, Yarran; do you also have meat here for the Tatya?"

"Most certainly not," scoffed Yarran. "Never will you see a day when the Leena hunt for the Tatya."

"You have more than you need, their need is much, and they are to provide honey," insisted Nalon.

"They are repaying a debt and the extra meat we have can be dried," replied Yarran. "I see no waste here. Baiame could not provide so we have provided for ourselves. Besides, the Tatya are not meat-eaters."

"Do you know that the Tatya clan are clever at thievery?" redirected Nalon of the conversation.

"I know this," said Yarran. "But we are many hunters with many pairs of eyes."

"Where there is the will to cheat another, the Tatya will find a way," said Nalon. "Would you jeopardise the friendship which has started to form between your two peoples, just to have more meat than you require."

"They will not eat meat, so what is the problem?" said Yarran.

"Every clan eats meat," said Nalon. "One who thieves also lies."

"This may be true, but it matters not, for we will not give any over," said Yarran and he turned into the column of hunters as they headed back to the Leena camp.

By the time all of the hunters had returned with their meat the Tatya had built a big fire amidst the stare of many women.

Derain greeted Yarran as he came upon his place. Derain had a hunter either side of him, coolamons filled with honey. "This is for you, Yarran, and there are many others awaiting your men, and some for the meat."

"Very good," said Yarran. "Thank you."

"You and your men appear tired. Why not rest and allow my men to cook the meat and place honey over it?" said Derain, smiling. "I hear it tastes wonderful."

Yarran recalled what Nalon had said and decided to be wary of the Tatya. "There will be no need. We will do the work."

"Very well," said Derain. "But please accept this, a selection of meat that your women prepared for you. We found a pygmy-possum not so far away and decided to capture it for you: we then gave it to one of your women. The honey will serve it well: a taste of things to come, just for you to try."

"As there is plenty for my men I shall accept this for myself," said Yarran and he ate the whole lot, and shortly after, being tired and full of good food, Yarran fell asleep.

Derain saw Nalon and Kalti beside Yarran, and he approached them. "Who are you that should be in the company of the Leena but not give aid to the hunt?"

"I am Nalon and this man is Kalti," said Nalon.

"Ah, Yes; I have heard of you," said Derain before laughing lightly. "It is said that you represent Baiame and that you are on walkabout, seeing the laws of the land, the laws of the creator, awoken: refreshed as it were. Yes; I have heard of you."

"But yet you still behave in a poorly manner," said Nalon.

"I have done nothing wrong; my people have done nothing wrong," said Derain.

"You lie and steal," said Nalon. "Is not that poor enough?"

"Have you seen me lie? Have you seen me steal? I think not."

"What I see and what I know are vision and instinct," said Nalon. "They may appear different but they are the same; but they are also as different from red berries and yellow yams."

"You make no sense, Nalon," said Derain. "Baiame must be a poor man to have sent you on errand."

"We see you act and know the play of your gestures; they orchestrate a similar tune; but beneath the facade we see a lie being performed to gain a reward and instinct states when a facade becomes transparent that the instinct is always correct. One man may see one combination of facets, but another will see something completely different. Perception is blurred beyond reason and conjectures give rise to faults. Yesterday yarran saw Ganan perform truth and considered him honest; today he sees contempt and feels violated by hidden agendas."

"Well, maybe you are right," said Derain. "But if it is for lessons you wish to see on your walkabout then look no further and I shall reward your courtesy. Look yonder and you will see my men going about the camp, helping the Leena to their mats for sleep. Only the women watch ever wakeful, each one seeing the illusion which they take as the truth. You see how the hunters of the Tatya put two pygmy-possums into the coals with their tails sticking out close together: this is for good reason, which you shall see later. The Leena are so sleepy and we cook the meat. How quickly they have forgotten in their tiredness that we have supposedly never cooked meat before this day. They appear ever thankful, their eyes growing heavy in the smoke. And now, look there, the last of the hunters falls to sleep and we, the Tatya, prepare what will be ours."

"You take from the hard work of others," said Nalon.

"Which is more sinful; to take freely from another, or to indulge in the unlawful killing of creation?" asked Derain.

"Both are equal, depending on the scenario," said Nalon.

"They are different I tell you and our theft is less unlawful," insisted Derain.

"Both are theft; both are sinful; but each is weighed differently, and yours in this case is much weightier," said Nalon. "The Tatya are exhausted, their source of nourishment depleted, yet you take from them knowing this, knowing they will not be able to gather more too soon. This is the same as forcing deprivation upon them, for many of the young will go without good sustenance; and even so, the laws of the land are changing and eating meat is not altogether a sin towards the law. Thievery will always be against the law but fair trade will always be embraced and encouraged."

"I do what I can to serve my clan," insisted Derain.

"You are scavengers," said Kalti. "If you do this thing you will be nothing more than foul creatures."

"The fouler we are the more capable of performing our errands," said Derain, and turned and walked away.

Nalon and Kalti did nothing more than sit there and watch as the hunters of the Leena fell asleep to the last, the women taking cover into their shelters, and the men of the Tatya cooking the meat, most of them moving into the trees for good vantage point over the Leena.

After darkness fell upon the land the meat was ready and along with this the Tatya descended from the trees and moved amongst the women who had come out to see the result of the cooked pygmy-possum with honey.

The Tatya were very calm and collective as they moved round into position and once there was a hunter covered off two pygmy-possum tails they leant forward and grabbed two tails to each man.

One of the women considered the actions extremely suspicious and gave alarm to several members of her clan who, themselves, woke up from their slumber to see what the matter was.

As the men of the Leena stirred the men of the Tatya grabbed the pygmy-possums and raced off into the forest, to lose the hunters in the dark, but the smell of meat was easy to follow.

The hunters of the Leena found it less cumbersome to chase with a spear than it was for a member of the Tatya to evade with two pygmy-possums in the hand, and it wasn't long before each of the men from Tatya took to the trees to hide. But they were soon surrounded and Yarran arrived at the foot of the trees which harboured the enemy and their food. But Derain did not manage to reach the trees.

Several men of the Leena, including the chief, had turned a branch each from the fire and held this in their hands. It was then that Derain raced up a tree next to the fire, the only means he saw available for him to escape the men surrounding him.

"Come down, Derain," ordered Yarran. "Come down now and save face, for you have done wrong by me and my clan. You must face punishment, to be delivered by me of my choosing, and decided upon by me alone."

Derain had not considered the ironic situation, for he and his clan had been cornered like the pygmy-possum they had endeavoured to cheat from their adversaries.

Derain came down from up there in the tree along with the other members of his clan who, although further away from the fire, descended down into the clutches of the Leena. There was then a horrific outlandish uproar from all and Leena men beat down hard upon the head and bodies of the Tatya who quickly dropped their pygmy-possums and ran off into the darkness.

Derain was not so lucky. Brandishing sticks with burnt ends the Leena closest to him, including Yarran, beat him senseless, all over the head and body until welts formed upon him, the ends of the sticks doing great damage to his body until he was covered in a camouflage of colour from ash to charcoal.

"That is enough!" commanded Nalon. "You have metered your punishment but the punishment is not just. He is a scavenger, nothing more. He crawls upon the ground like a creature: look at him. He is vile, he is worthless. He climbs trees and steals from others; he eats meat, and would do so even if the meat was already decaying."

The wirinum of the Leena spoke up: "What shall become of him and his people? They cannot be left to steal again. What justice will the great Baiame deliver?"

And Nalon put his arms to the sky and commanded: "From this day forth the clan of the Tatya shall resemble the creatures so explicitly described." And in the thunderous clap of thunder form above the hunters – and the Tatya women folk back at their camp – to the last were transformed into hideous goannas.

The Tatya looked bewildered at their new look, the goannas scrambling away on all four legs, scurrying away to hide under a log or to climb up high into a tree.

"As the Madhi were turned to dingoes, so the Tatya are turned to goannas, and so will their lives be forever changed for the good of all creation."

THE BOOMERANG

Nalon and Kalti stood upon the verge of land between the forest and the plains. It was early morning.

"You should be careful to cross this open land," said Yarran.

"We shall skirt it for a while," said Nalon, "before making a decision of final destination. But we go where we are needed most."

"My people and I thank you," said Yarran.

"There is only one way in which you can truly thank me," said Nalon. "And I believe you know the way."

"You want that we should change our ways," said Yarran. "I wish I could, for you have more than proven your worth and the laws of Baiame. But what are we to do?"

"I will be happy to make a compromise," said Nalon.

"Please, tell me."

"I had the idea when I showed you the Gayandi," said Nalon.

"Ah, yes; a great gift indeed," said Yarran, smiling.

"Well, when I looked down upon it, and understanding the way in which it moved through the air, did decide upon this." And when he lifted his hand he was holding something like a flat piece of wood with a bend in it. "I call this a boomerang."

"A boomerang," repeated Yarran as he took it from Nalon and weighed it in his grasp.

"It is used for hunting. With this you can take what you need in order to sustain you hunger, but maintain equilibrium in nature in order for it to sustain itself; it will be useful against the kyeema, that which was created by Yowie. You must never completely decimate your food source, unless it is from one of the creatures so known to have been created by Yowie."

"How do I use it?" asked Yarran.

Nalon took it from him. "Let me show you." And as though in slow motion, Nalon threw the boomerang away from him and it returned, back into the palm of his hand. "With practise your people will become proficient."

"Thank you again," said Yarran. "And if there is anything you need in the future, please send us smoke and I shall see it. I shall have a man, always, watching for your signal."

And with those last words being spoken both Nalon and Kalti continued with their walkabout.

They had found a friend, being on the verge between forest and plains, who would always be in reach of a good smoke signal.

THE FISHING NET

The journey into the west was hard, the heat almost unbearable and no water to be had anywhere. There were small scrub, saltbush, and trees scattered here and there: mainly acacia, and boab.

"Maybe you can make water," suggested Kalti.

"Water comes from clouds and clouds come from Baiame," said Nalon. "I do not know how to make clouds as I am limited in my powers. Those ordained by the Great Father are considered necessities."

"I am thirsty," said Kalti. "Is that necessary? Is it not permitted to quench this thirst?"

"The Spirit of Death will be waiting," said Nalon. "Any action by me can be counter actioned by the Yowie. To give more leash to him than is required will see further calamity here on what we know to be the earth; and earth and sky-land are two different realms."

"And what of the pygmy-possums?" asked Kalti as the continued walking over the plains and away from the forest.

"Yes, it is true," considered Nalon. "I should consider the option to replenish what has been culled, for the overwhelming loss. I can only hope that Yarran will learn something of what has happened so that nature can reap reward."

And for the next half a day they continue on until they saw a silhouette of something upon the horizon.

Kalti looked at Nalon and could see that he, too, saw it. "What do you think it is?"

"It is very far away, but it looks like trees; very fat trees, like bulbs growing above the ground instead of within it."

"Maybe we should ask the Great Father Spirit for advice," said Kalti.

"Again, we cannot," said Nalon. "We have all been granted the ability to think, the greatest gift that Baiame could provide us. When we get close enough we will know what it is and what to do."

It was then that they first came face to face with the most monstrous of beasts that they had ever seen. Before them both were a beast that looked like a goanna but it was four times the length of a man, from head to tip of tail, weighed in excess of eight men, and was capable of bringing down and eating a mallee-akana.

From out of nowhere and hidden by a saltbush, a voice came upon their ears from some distance away, voiced loud enough for them to be drawn upon it. The large and monstrous lizard also heard the noise and turned its monstrous head, away from Nalon and Kalti.

"Do not move," said the voice once more. "I shall draw the pindoola [*Pindan-Oola*: desert (male) – red lizard (female): lizard of the desert – a fabricated name for a megalania] away from you and kill it."

"I shall give you aid," said a confident Kalti and as he did so the pindoola snapped its monstrous head back to view its next meal.

Kalti moved slowly and readied his spear before him as the pindoola stepped leisurely forward in preparation for a lunge and quick snap of the jaws with huge teeth which were dripping with saliva.

The man with the voice of warning now stepped from hiding and came to view a full pindoola body length away: Nalon stood still and watched, learning what he could, weapon-less to defend himself.

"Here; over here," yelled the man, drawing the attention of the pindoola.

"You are confusing it," said Kalti, the pindoola snapping its head back once more.

"And you too, friend," said the young man. "Keep it up."

"I shall," replied Kalti, and together they drew closer and closer to the confused beast until they were approaching from either side of it, and fearing as though it was trapped the pindoola turned and fled away.

The young man relaxed and his throwing hand, with spear, lowered its threat. Kalti did the same and all three men came together.

"My name is Kalti, and this is Nalon," said Kalti. "Thank you for helping us like that."

"My name is Mogo [a stone axe], for I am said to be efficient with that weapon."

"We are pleased to meet you," said Nalon.

"Nalon; I have heard of that name, and so too has the wirinum, I am sure," said Mogo. "We had heard a message upon the wind of a new weapon called the boomerang."

"The wind must travel fast," said Nalon. "It is a new invention, only recently called into service for the people, to give aid to those that hunt."

"Our wirinum is powerful of mind and can see words as well as hear them," said Mogo.

"What is his name?" asked Nalon. "Maybe I know him."

"His name is Konol [the sky]," said Mogo.

"As true a wirinum name as any," admitted Nalon, "but I have never heard of him."

"We came this way when food went scarce," advised Mogo, "and since then have been waging a war against the Spirit of Death."

"You have heard about much," said Nalon.

"We have men who travel far and wide, to return with news from many quarters," admitted Mogo. "It also makes for good trade."

"What is the name of you clan?" asked Nalon.

"We are called the Lurnea [resting place] clan, and my chief is Orad [earth], for he loves the land on which the Great Father Spirit has given to us."

"And what do you trade?" asked Nalon.

"We trade teeth," said Mogo to a shocked look of despair. "Do not fear; not the teeth of men, but the teeth of the pindoola. They make for good weapons."

"But you seem to use a spear," pointed out Kalti.

"Teeth make reasonable weapons: clubs, knives, axes; but it has little range. The spear is the best weapon. Besides, we always trade the teeth for shells, berries and yams, and sometimes pandanus leaves."

"Pandanus?" questioned Nalon.

"Come," invited Mogo, with a smile. "I will show you, but first we must get to camp and eat."

After much walking they came upon a beautiful place where gum trees grew along slightly sloping ground: before them was a monstrous inland sea of fresh water. There were lilies galore nearer some of the banks and it seemed as though the lake was teeming with birdlife.

"We call this great place Araluen [the place of waterlilies]," said Mogo, kissing the wind and indicating the vastness that filled their eyes.

"I have never seen such a thing as this," said Nalon with a smile.

"I too, am simply breath taken," added Kalti.

"It allows us to survive," said Mogo. "We fish and then eat the catch, and we believe with all our heart that this is permitted by the Great Father Spirit for there is also many kurria here."

"So, he has found a way," said Nalon, understanding how Pikuwa, after being turned into a kurria, had ventured far and wide.

"Who has found a way?" asked Mogo.

"The Spirit of Death, Mogo," said Nalon. "For I imprisoned a man named Pikuwa into a cage of hardened flesh and called him kurria. It is clear to me now that the Spirit of Death has come and provided him with a female."

"There number is not too great," said Mogo, "and they are very little at the present, but growing larger each day. They eat the fish that appeared from the sky and so we, too, eat them. If a creature such as this can eat… well, then why should we not?" stated Mogo. "First we fed on roots and berries, upon the crests and other sources so abundant as provided by this great water, but herbivores so large came upon us and devoured much. We had no choice to try and take from them. We hunt them, too, regardless of their size, and do well at it."

"I believe you," said Nalon, "for you have already demonstrated how you can handle a pindoola."

Mogo smiled and then lead them further, along the bank and close to the water. They passed a tree and Mogo pointed out across the water with his lips. There before them could be seen a miracle. There were two men floating upon the water. Then the turbulence upon the surface revealed that the men were actually sitting upon a dug out log and as it turned it revealed something sticking up from it.

"What is that?" asked Nalon.

"I shall tell you," said Mogo. "Those two men are Warra [water] and Bardo [water], and they invented this thing called a sail which catches the wind. In the beginning it was meant simply as a branch with leaves, stuck in a hole within the canoe to provide shade from the hot sun whilst on the water, but the men soon realised that the wind would sometimes drag them across the water because of the sail. As the leaves upon the branch died so did the amount of acceleration across the water and so Bardo fell upon the idea of using pandanus leaves woven between the branches to capture the wind. What do you think of this invention, Nalon?

Mogo seemed so proud that his clan could muster such thought as to invent something so useful. "It is a wondrous thing, Mogo," said Nalon. "I am sure that with time you will find further use for this… sail."

"I hope so, too," said Mogo. "Come, follow me and I shall introduce you to the other members of the clan."

And true to his word both Nalon and Kalti followed Mogo a short distance to their camp where introduction was made.

The Lurnea clan maintained much law and order within; its chief and wirinum were proud and happy men.

Nalon made a request, which was acknowledged: he wanted to meet the men who had made the sail; but it was not until late that Warra and Bardo fell upon the camp, very wet but with two fish each.

It was quickly explained to Nalon that the catch was the limit for a good day upon the water, for even with the aid of the canoe and the sail the fishing was hard.

"Warra, Bardo," said Orad. "Nalon would be pleased to see the sail. Would you be able to take him to it when the sun rises?"

"We are sorry, Orad," said Warra, "but the sail is missing.

"Whatever happened?" asked Orad.

"A wind; very strong; much stronger than normal in fact, came upon us and snatched it from its secure post. It was flung into the water and quickly drifted away towards the bank. We shall look for it in the morning."

"Very well," said the chief, a little disappointed.

"Could I please come with you?" asked Nalon.

"Of course," said Bardo. "Both you and Kalti are welcome."

The following morning, and after a good meal of edible roots and tubers, the four men stepped out of the camp and made their way towards the bank of the Araluen.

"I think if we look around here we will find the sail," said Bardo.

"Is it safe to wade in the water with so many kurria about?" asked Kalti.

"They do not come to this area in the morning, for they find more to eat in other areas," advised Bardo. "It is quite safe to do so."

And so Nalon waded in the water alongside Warra, with Bardo and Kalti walking alongside upon the bank.

They had not gone far when Warra found what they were looking for. "There it is," he said, pointing with his lips kissing the air. "It seems to be strung up upon a snag of that gum tree."

Warra moved forward and grabbed at the sail and to his astonishment found something more.

He was shocked and overjoyed. "Look!" he yelled. "Look at this!"

The other three were quick to join him and to their astonishment they saw what Warra saw. There were five fish caught up within the sail.

"How can this be possible," pronounced Bardo.

"Look," said Nalon. "The cross sections and interlocking frame work of the sticks and the pandanus have acted like a... like a net for fishing."

"A net for fishing," repeated Warra.

"A fishing net," said Kalti.

"And it has snared more fish by just sitting here than we could catch in a day upon the water with our spears," said Bardo.

The four men were quick to take the news back to the chief who immediately set Warra and Bardo upon the task of making a larger and better net with the pandanus that they had remaining.

"We need more pandanus," said the chief as he smiled.

"I shall get some more," said Mogo happily. "I shall go with some of the teeth from the hunt and get some more pandanus."

"Good, Mogo," said the chief. "Soon we will be able to trade with fish, for fish will be more valuable than mere trinkets."

"I know of a small lagoon," said Warra. "It is close to Araluen and we can store any excess fish here. We can place a net of pandanus at the thin mouth between the two so that the fish will not escape. We could then kill the fish as we need them."

"A very good idea," said Orad. "We shall also need to keep a watch upon it, for the kurria will try and take fish from it."

"Bardo and I shall be glad to take turns in remaining between the two waters, until better arrangements can be made."

"Good," said the chief. "Mogo, take what you need and be back as soon as you can so that we can benefit from this thing called a fishing net."

And Mogo departed soon after.

BROTHER POSSUM

As Mogo went upon his way he passed by the hiding spot of a middle aged man who was watching unseen. His name was Dural [a hollow tree that is on fire]. Mogo passed him by without noticing him and Dural then came out of hiding and moved on towards the small lagoon of no real distinction. He saw Warra and Bardo placing the finishing touches to the screen of pandanus. He quietly hid himself once more.

"That should do it," said Warra. "All we need to do now is place the live fish in the lagoon and harvest the supply as we require it."

"You can start by placing these fish into it," said the chief as an entourage of women from behind him came up and deposit many fish into the lagoon. "We now have fish to eat and time to prepare for a special ceremony in honour of this thing called a fishing net."

Dural watched as the fish were placed into the lagoon and everyone departed the area, but still he did not move.

Later that night he came out of hiding and moved to the edge of the lagoon and saw that it was thick with fish. He simply placed his hands into the water and pulled out a large fish, as large as he had ever seen in his entire life.

Dural scurried away, covering his tracks as he moved across the plain with the leafy branch of a tree which he carried in his left hand, the fish in his right, and at a safe distance from the Lurnea, at a small clump of bushes and trees, he built himself a fire and cooked his meal. He was so satisfied by what he ate that he fell asleep almost immediately, dreaming upon the next day when he would put up a shelter and continue his life as a hermit.

The next day, after having made himself a shelter and permanent hearth, Dural went to see about getting another fish. As he approached he heard a slapping noise. He moved closer.

Warra was hitting the surface of the water with what appeared to be a flat paddle, hence scaring the fish which then jumped out of the water and rushed around in the cramped surrounds of their watery prison. Bardo stood knee deep and scooped up some fish.

Bardo, on climbing out, looked at Warra. "There are many fish here; you can see how many by the contrast of open space between the bodies of the fish as they swim around. I would call this amount a very large amount indeed."

"I agree," said Warra. "And now it is time to get back."

Once again Dural came out from hiding and approached the lagoon, but this time he helped himself to three fish, for his stomach was stretching and he was hungry from sitting around and doing nothing all day: but thinking of eating fresh fish. He was a recluse but now he was a thief as well.

The Lurnea did not take any more fish for an entire week for they had other resources which they had available to them, and knowing that the fish stock would always be on hand to take when they needed it they considered it best to keep them in reserve.

By the seventh day Dural was taking six fish each day in order to keep him full, the remainder of his time he remained asleep, he also slept during the day but fed by night when he discovered that the fish were easier to catch. He had become nocturnal in all his behaviours.

Now, on the seventh day of not touching the fish, Warra and Bardo approached the lagoon to take enough of their prize to feed the clan. When they arrived they were shocked to find that there was only a third of the fish left, swimming around at their leisure.

"What has happened?" expressed Warra of his concern, his open mouth suggestive of his shock. "Where have the fish gone?"

"It cannot be the kurria, or any other meat eating animal, for we have always had someone watching Araluen."

"We should inform Orad immediately and see what he has to say," said Warra, and so they departed the lagoon and reported to the chief what they had found.

"Yes," agreed Bardo. "But check the pandanus screen first for any holes and the trees for any sign of a large bird or two."

Orad was very discouraged to hear that the fish were gone. "Maybe the screen is broken, or there might be a large bird about," he suggested.

"No," said Bardo. "We checked. We also looked for animal tracks and there is nothing at all to be seen. The nearest animal track leads straight past the lagoon and to Araluen."

"May I suggest something?" interrupted Nalon, politely.

"Of course," said Orad. "We would be happy to hear your thoughts."

"During our time together I have learnt much about your ways and have also noticed how honest your transaction and communications between one another are. You are sincere people and uphold the laws of Baiame as best you can, and neither do you interrupt in the lives of those creatures which do not harm you," said Nalon. "I can therefore see only one alternative to this dilemma and that is of an unknown in our presence who is taking from the lagoon without permission."

"You mean," stared Orad, "someone other than our clan?"

"Yes," said Nalon. "I can only suggest that we watch the lagoon carefully over the next few days, from a distance, and see what we can discover of this problem."

So Warra and Bardo set themselves the task of watching the lagoon together, one asleep and one always awoke, watching and waiting, waiting and watching. And when the sun went down Warra heard a noise for Dural was approaching with his leafy branch in one hand and the other rubbing his stomach.

Warra woke Bardo gently and both watched earnestly to see what was to happen, and they did not have to wait long. Dural was quick to catch eight fish from within the lagoon and turned to leave.

Suddenly Warra and Bardo jumped out of hiding and captured Dural as he squirmed and squealed, trying with his entire mite to get away.

"You have been stealing our fish," accused Warra, correctly. "And you shall pay for your crime."

"You are a dishonest man," said Bardo, "and a thief, through and through."

Dural could say nothing in return for it was all true and he had been caught red handed.

The commotion of the capture and the thrashing of Dural on the return to camp awoke all of those within. Every person stood up to see what the matter was, congregating around the centre fire of the clan and waiting for Warra and Bardo to deposit their captive amongst them.

Dural was surrounded and there was no way in which he could escape.

Orad heard from Warra and Bardo, and that was enough for him to scold Dural. "You should be ashamed of yourself. You are our brother," said Orad, "a man in semblance to us, one created by the Great Father Spirit himself. But you have turned to thievery and taken what is ours, knowing full well that you are doing an injustice to us."

"I am sorry," cried Dural. "But I was hungry. I live alone and have no one to help me gather good food. I only took what I needed in order to survive."

"You are a thief and a liar," cried Nalon from the back as he pushed his way gently to the front in order to be seen by everyone. "You are a recluse of this land; you have adapted yourself to sleeping by day and eating by night. You actions are callous and enacted with deliberate purpose."

"He shall be punished," ordered Orad.

"Yes," voiced Kalti. "But by the grace of Nalon, he will be treated in accordance to his lifestyle."

"And what do you mean by that?" asked Orad. Nalon, too, looked at Kalti for an answer.

"You recall the problem with the Leena, Nalon, and the pygmy-possum," stated Kalti. "The pygmy-possum is endangered, near extinction, and yet this world created by Baiame is so young. Maybe you should consider doing with Dural as you did with Pikuwa and the Tatya."

Nalon considered this and looked at the chief. "If it would please, Orad, I shall enact punishment upon Dural which will see him routed from here to the forest lands forever, to live his life for eternity as he has lead it these past eight days."

"That seems fitting," said Orad. "But will he not be a burden to others?"

"No," said Nalon, "for he will become a vermin to be hunted by those that seek to eat meat."

"We eat fish to take from the kurria, to gnaw on the flesh of these fish which were a gift," said Orad. "We cannot be compared to those that eat pygmy-possums."

"Each and every clan has its own way; this is what I am learning." said Nalon. "The Lurnea are as good a people as are the Leena, and having nothing further to say I shall now enact the punishment fitting to the crimes of Dural."

And Nalon uplifted his hands and dropped them again, Dural turning into a possum, much larger than a pygmy-possum.

"You shall feed the world and live as you have lived these past few days," ordered Nalon. "And to ensure to get to where you are destined to go I have provided you with good reason, for in the land of the Leena there is now a female possum waiting for you, to accept you with open arms."

And Dural, now a possum, looked up into the eyes of Nalon before scurrying away.

"If I did not know any better," said Kalti. "I would swear that Dural just gave you thanks for what you have done."

"And why should he not," said Nalon, "for I have given him life and a wife."

Nalon stood there with Kalti; Orad, Warra and Bardo were there, too. Mogo moved up beside them all.

"Mogo will go with you," said Orad, "as far as the next rise which you can see in the distance. You should be there by the time the sun is at its highest."

Nalon nodded assent. "Thank you, Orad."

Mogo then looked at Orad, his chief. "If it would please my chief I would like to make a request."

"Please," said Orad. "Continue."

"I am a trader, and new partners in trade would be a benefit to us all," started Mogo. "I would therefore ask if I may go with Nalon and Kalti, to the edge of the world, to take this walkabout into my heart and to learn from it."

Nalon said: "You wish to learn of the Dreamtime. You wish to experience this walkabout, and experience the creation of this world."

"Yes," said Mogo. "That is it."

Orad looked at Nalon, Kalti and Mogo, in turn, with a smile upon his face. "Is that what it is called, Nalon? Is this Dreamtime you speak about a part of us?"

"It is everything," said Nalon. "Without Dreamtime you would not exist, and our walkabout will uncover all there is to learn of Dreamtime, for the benefit of all. A walkabout should be experienced as an individual, but as there is so much to learn, and as I see no reason to stretch the boundaries of spiritual awareness to the complete discovery of Dreamtime and the creation of everything, I think that just this once we can walkabout together."

"Then I envy you all," said Orad, "and bid you good walking."

The three men turned away and recommenced their walkabout, one which had started with a single step from a single man and now encompassed an unfinished journey with three men, each in the good company of the other.

ARINYA

The clan was a small clan of no name. It had no name for it was young and unskilled in the art of ceremony, whether cooroboree or other, for one was more sacred than the other.

The chief was Jarrah [a type of eucalyptus] who was strong and wise. He ruled with a smile always upon his face and always allowed others to have their say in most matters concerning the transition of their small clan from its brash underlying past to a bold and encouraging future.

The wirinum was Pindar [from the high ground] who had been provided his station as medicine man for his wise and collective outlook on bringing ceremony to life, where the good spirits of the camp came alive by night, each and every one of the clan learning to live with nature one day and then cull it the next.

And last but not least a good clan required a good hunter and in this the clan they had Miro [a throwing stick] who was extremely apt at throwing a spear; and who very seldom missed a target: it was said that the spirit of the Great Father was always with him.

And so it came to pass that Nalon and his good company fell upon the fire of the camp as they sat round it in good spirits, now and again getting up to perform a dance and cause music to fill the air through the use of musical instruments such as clapping two sticks together or blowing through the didjeridu [didgeridoo], and singing from deep down within the throat, reverberating sound which echoed loud and fair, most symbolic and beautiful.

The dancers around the fire stopped, but not in unison, and the chief turned to stare upon the arrival of Nalon, Kalti and Mogo: to whom Nalon gave introduction in order for the clan to see that they were friendly.

Suddenly there was much celebration and chatter as the clan folded around the visitors, seeing that they were few and harmless.

"I have heard the name Nalon," said Jarrah, "upon the wind as it blows, although so seldom from the east."

"I hope that the wind does me favour," said Nalon.

"If it had not then we would be greeting you with the tip of our spears at your belly," said Miro, and the throng laughed out loud.

They were all soon seated and a small meal upon bark was placed before the three walkers, who ate politely.

"Do you have a story to tell, Nalon?" asked Pindar, most anxious to hear good word and teaching.

"The laws of the land must be reinstated to their former glory," said Nalon as Mogo and Kalti nodded assent. "Baiame is not pleased with the actions each clan is taking towards its own growth and survival. Many laws are being broken, but also there is hope, for many new ceremonies and sacred cooroboree are being fuelled, and so there is reason to be optimistic."

"I have heard that a law of killing certain animals has been lifted," suggested Jarrah of something he was not sure.

"There is much confusion upon the land for hunger is widespread," said Nalon, not replying to the question directly. "The Spirit of Evil has been defeated but the spirit of Death is upon the land, and he is driving the clans to unlawful existence. There are many creations upon the earth that now ravage and plunder all there is to eat, but worse still, some are designed to eat meat."

"I saw one not long ago," said Miro. "It was a great lizard like none I have ever seen before."

"It is called a pindoola," said Kalti, "and I have killed one."

Half of those listening draw back their breath, the exclamation of great wonder and surprise being heard by all.

"They are hard to kill," said Kalti.

"The Spirit of Death is Yowie," said Nalon. "He has created many vermin, with the aid of the former Spirit of Evil, to enact great treason upon Baiame and his good nature. Monstrous beasts and small insects alike are destroying the land and turning it to dust, and now Yowie creates creatures that will eat man, one and all. The direction we choose to take in this life is a hard one to make but laws must be adhered to where possible, for Baiame created us all."

"I understand what you are saying," said Jarrah. "As we all do. Take that meat you have eaten. It is the meat of a beast of nature so vicious that it is hard to fathom. He is called Dingo."

Nalon passed visual contact with Kalti and Mogo, each glancing upon the other so that the chief of the clan could see that something was the matter.

"You know of this animal; clearly it has surprised you," said Jarrah.

"This one we know," said Nalon. "Though not for some time have I seen it personally. I do know from whence it came."

"Tell us," urged Jarrah.

"It is a creation of... Baiame. The dingoes are those sodden men and women known as the Madhi clan. It is their torment to tread this land on four legs as opposed to two for their heinous misgivings."

"I did not know," said Pindar in an apologetic manner to Jarrah.

"So," pried jarrah of an answer. "Is eating dingo against the law as granted the land?"

"It is not strictly forbidden," started Nalon, "for no law has been passed upon it, but it would be distasteful to eat another man or woman, and so to eat the meat of a dingo is not something to be considered lightly."

"You think it cannibalistic?" asked Jarrah.

"Yes and no," said Nalon. "I have not given it much thought."

And the silence upon the camp that followed was very strange, so strange that an animal close by could not understand the matter with the situation and so his curiosity got the better of him.

117

The kyeema came out of hiding and stepped into the arena where men and women had been dancing. He was not afraid of man for he had never encountered man before. The kyeema did not know that danger was present and the curiosity within him could not be stifled.

The members of the clan turned and looked, all silent and in a state of half shock, for they had seen a kyeema before, but never had one entered their camp.

Nalon was as mystified as anyone else and watched closely.

Suddenly a noise came from its flank and it turned with a hop. The kyeema then hopped away in a great hurry, for a woman had stumbled out from the tree line where she had been toileting and had scared it.

Miro stood up and grabbed his spear. "Quickly, we must be after it."

"No," said Jarrah. "It is too dark. We shall chase him down on the morrow."

Pindar then stood up and looked around him at all the others gathered. The sky above was sparkling with bright stars and several insects could be heard in the far distance. Slowly the wirinum lifted his left leg and thrust his foot down into the ground and looked around at his audience. He then lifted his right and did the same, a little dust billowing up as his foot struck the ground. He turned his head to look in the other direction but did it so quickly, just like the kyeema had done.

He stopped. "This is the kyeema dance," said Pindar. "This is a sacred moment to be remembered: the day we were visited by the great kyeema. And we shall call him Arinya. He has challenged us, and on the morrow we shall defeat him, but right now we shall dance to his existence, to celebrate his arrival. And on the night following his death we shall celebrate further with full stomachs and happy faces."

The people around got up and joined in on the new dance which had been created.

Nalon looked at the chief of the clan. "You have no name, but now I say you do. You are the Arinya clan."

"Yes," said Jarrah, chin up. "We are the Arinya."

BURRAJAHNEE AND INNEROOGUN

The following day saw the Arinya and Nalon with his company, on the hunt. They were after the Kyeema who had so boldly entered into the ceremony of the cooroboree: a forward party of trap setters were far ahead of them and had been dispatched before dawn.

As the hunting was underway the spectacle was seen from high above where an old man named Jerara [falling water] and his nephew [Nioka, meaning 'green hills'] gazed down upon them from the plateau, which was so situated that a large waterfall existed and drowned out the sound of everything around them. With them they had two dingoes, dingoes of the Madhi who had separated from the clan, the clan having dispersed into smaller groups soon after their transformation into dingoes. The dingoes were called Burrajahnee and Inneroogun.

The dingoes were more mystified by the hunting party than the men and saw, with great excitement, the kyeema they were hunting as it dashed past their view. The kyeema swept past them, halfway between the two parties, changing direction and moving down the slope alongside the waterfall towards a nearby lagoon, and before the old man and his nephew could issue a command the two dingoes were off after the kyeema.

Jerara and Nioka cried out for the dingoes to halt but to no avail, for nothing could be heard over the crashing of the waterfall.

Meanwhile the forward element of the hunting party had set two traps. Both were made in a similar fashion to the fishing nest made of pandanus, for Nalon had introduced them to it the night before.

The kyeema came up upon the first trap and saw before him a large net made of vines, stretched out across the path to his front, a track that he had used many times in the past. It was at this same time that the kyeema heard the sound of the charging dingoes behind him as they came snapping at his heels before the kyeema placed more effort into his jumps and accelerated away from those chasing him.

So fast was the kyeema travelling that he simply tore through the first trap with no effort at all, but leaving such destruction behind him also permitted easy chase for the dingoes, who once again gained a little ground upon him.

The second trap then came to view, a surprise more than anything else, and leaping over it the kyeema clipped his toes upon the upper vines and tumbled head over tail to land in the lagoon not so far away.

Two points of interest occurred at this moment, all of which were as important to the other, for each had the power to change the history of all the clans that walked the earth as seen through the eyes of Baiame.

As the kyeema hit the surface of the water a monstrous enigmatic creature of robust and malicious form opened its jaws filled with sharp teeth and snatched unopposed onto the meal that had interrupted his slumber. It was to become known as the bunyip, a creature so fearsome and unpredictable, a cast of creature that was something between a burna-korra and a mallee-akana, but with the menacing jaws of a pindoola. This was a description given by one of the frightened men who saw a glimpse of the attack from his hiding place within the tree line, a second of visual contact which was quickly drawn to the next event.

Both Burrajahnee and Inneroogun had been snared by the second trap, the movement of the kyeema over the top of it forcing the supporting vine to fall, the net collapsing upon them both. They struggled for a few moments but without second thought another hunter dashed out from hiding and thrust the point of his spear into the hearts of the dingoes, killing them instantly, and an act of unnecessary weight in the eyes of Jerara and Nioka.

Once the Arinya had returned to their camp the chief gathered everyone around and stories of the hunt filled the air and of particular interest was the bunyip.

"What do you say to this?" asked Jarrah, of Nalon.

"It is a fierce creature, to be sure," replied Nalon. He looked at Kalti but Kalti seemed as lost as he.

"But have you no knowledge of such a thing?" asked the chief.

"No," replied Nalon.

"And you, Pindar, wirinum of the Arinya," asked Jarrah. "What do you know of this thing called bunyip? Surely you must know something."

"No, Jarrah," said Pindar. He looked to Miro. "You are a great hunter. What do you know of this thing?"

"I know nothing," confessed Miro. "If a wirinum, nor a representative of Baiame, can draw conclusion, how am I to derive knowledge?"

"You are a hunter," said Jarrah. "You have travelled these lands and killed many animals."

"But I have not been walking about," said Miro, looking now at Nalon, accusingly.

"I shall think upon this thing," said Nalon, and drew the only conclusion possible. "It seems to me to be a representative of evil, commanded into existence by Death, a manipulation of his previous creations to see fear put into the hearts of men. It must be Death; yes indeed. He has manifested into existence creatures to scour the land and deprive you of food, and now he has created a creature which will forever deprive you of fresh water, for I see in your eyes the fear invoked. This fear, if not controlled, will see you all tremble at the thought of approaching any source of water, be it a river, a stream, lagoon, lake or billabong."

"What can we do, Nalon?" asked Jarrah.

"Do nothing," said he. "Be cunning and ever watchful, and above all, be wise."

"Yes, that is the answer," said Jarrah. "And now, in light of the catch that we have before us we should feast."

"You should not temp the fury of a thing you do not know, by devouring such a source of nourishment that should not be consumed," said Nalon.

"It is meat," said Jarrah. "A creation of punishment, of reprimand, lashed out to the Madhi clan for unlawful behaviour. It should be fitting to see them hunted and killed, withdrawn from the land."

"They have reason now," said Nalon. "They have something to offer men, hunting instincts that will give you aid, not distress, misfortune or nuisance. They may aid you in your survival against the Bunyip."

"Well," started Jarrah, "we shall see. But these two animals here shall be eaten, for they have already been denied life."

And without further ado the clan made preparations for skinning, cooking, and eating the two dingoes, Burrajahnee and Inneroogun.

It was night and Nalon, Kalti and Mogo were standing upon the edge of the clearing to the camp.

"It is well that we have not eaten of the dingo," said Nalon. "It is not the thing to do."

All three then turned their heads, away from the Arinya, who were all fast asleep with stomachs full of dingo meat. A sound had caught their ears; someone was approaching.

"It is time for us to depart," whispered Nalon as he stepped away and converged with the darkness around him. Kalti and Mogo looked upon one another and then followed.

Moments later and Jerara and Nioka stepped out silently from the direction of their approach.

"Look at this," said Jerara, seeing the bones of his two animals piled beside the camp fire. "This clan has eaten both Burrajahnee and Inneroogun. It is an insult to us as men."

"What shall we do?" asked Nioka, his youthful inexperience coming to air.

"We shall gather the bones and take them away, give them a descent ceremony for which to pass from this world to the next," said Jerara. "Maybe their spirit will come back as men, men who will torture this vile clan."

"Why do you not do it," urged Nioka. "You should act on their part; seek some manner of justice for Burrajahnee and Inneroogun. You use to be a wirinum of times past, before you left the Madhi to seek a wife."

"Yes," said Jerara. "And what good did it do me, for the wife died from hunger."

"But you have me in her place," said the nephew, his palm falling softly upon the shoulder of the old man. "The Madhi were your clan once, one that you held deep respect for. You should not let this act go unpunished. I shall stand by you."

"Thank you, Nioka," said Jerara. "I shall try and do what I can."

The two men gathered the bones of Burrajahnee and Inneroogun and moved away, and once out of hearing Jerara did cast his magic upon the vicinity, drawing revenge from the surrounds to fall upon the Arinya without mercy. The wind started to blow and the trees began to shake. Stronger and stronger became the wind and rustling of trees that its ferocity blew out the camp fire, and then within the strongest lashes of breeze that could be whipped up the wind snapped into action and blew away all remnant of the Arinya. All of the men, women and children of the clan, who had partaking in the flesh of the dingoes, did turn to ash and were blown away.

Jerara and Nioka had turned their backs upon the calamity and carried the bones away from the area, up the slope to the plateau, alongside the great waterfall which fed the plains below. And once at the top the bones were placed upon the ground, sorted into two piles, and with tears welled in their eyes both Jerara and Nioka turned to face different directions to give praise. And as they sat there the two piles of bones were turned to stone, forever reminders of the existence of Burrajahnee and Inneroogun; to be forever sacred.

THE ECHIDNA AND HIS SPINES

The three wise men had been walking for some time and had managed to bypass the monsters that covered the land so sparse that is seemed strange when falling upon a small herd. But continue on their walkabout they did.

One day, just a short time after the day in which the Arinya were dealt such a savage blow to their existence, the three fell upon a dry river bed, small but otherwise quite definite.

Mogo seemed to stop dead in his tracks as Nalon and Kalti crossed the ground which was easy to manage, its banks rather shallow.

"What is it, Mogo?" asked Nalon. "Why are you not crossing this dry river bed?"

"I cannot go any further," replied Mogo quite bluntly.

"But why?" searched Nalon of an answer.

"The lands beyond this river, so widely known by all traders that pass from clan to clan, know what exists beyond."

"What?" asked Kalti, mystified.

"We have just departed from the Arinya, who ate dingoes, but beyond this river you will be entering the land of cannibals," said Mogo. "I have travelled far and wide but only twice have I dared cross this river. The first time I was lucky to escape with my life, for there was an old man who appeared over anxious to have me sit before him at his fire. It was when I saw the human bones piled high beside his humpy that I ran for my life. The second time I was forced across in search of water when I fell upon another named Wahn. He too showed signs of untoward behaviour."

"Maybe you were mistake," urged Kalti.

"No," said Nalon, seeing the light. "You are quite right, Mogo; I see it now. But I must continue with my journey."

"And I must remain by your side," added Kalti.

"I am sorry, Nalon; I am sorry, Kalti; but my job is done and I can do no more," said Mogo as he turned around and walked off the other way, not a further word spoken.

"What shall we do now?" asked Kalti of Nalon.

"We shall continue as before and do as we are bid," replied Nalon, and they stepped off again in unison.

They had not gone far when they fell upon a small clan. They entered to find many men and women looking at them.

"Are they cannibalistic?" asked Kalti in a whisper.

"I should not think so," answered Nalon, "for I can see many bones, here and there, and all are of the beasts associated with Death; the burna-korra, mallee-akana, and pindoola."

A man approached them, a smile upon his face. "Greetings; please; I am Dorak [lively] the chief of the Manilla [a winding river] clan, so named for we are camped not far from what was once a running river."

"I see it," said Nalon. "I am Nalon and this is Kalti," and he continued to provide introduction as to their purpose.

"I will do justice to Baiame," said Dorak, "by offering you a place by our fire… something good to eat."

With this spoken, Kalti looked at Nalon with slight apprehension, hoping that the meaning of the words were not that he was the meal.

"Thank you, Dorak," said Nalon with a smile. "We humbly accept and hope to discuss much in regards to re-instating the laws of the land and learning of the nature of all clans who reside upon this side of the dry river."

"Certainly, it would be an honour."

All were sat around the fire at the centre of the camp having almost finished eating when a young and beautiful woman came and sat between two friends. The chief looked at her.

"Where is your husband, Carina [a bride]?" asked Dorak.

"Warrigal [wild] is always at the humpy," replied Carina.

"Are you to take him something to eat?" asked the chief.

"No," replied Carina. "For he does not wish for anything."

And then the wirinum requested something special.

"Carina; after we have eaten you might like to share your beautiful voice with us all and bring delight to our special audience of two. I am sure both Nalon and Kalti would love to hear the beautiful sounds from within that you make so well."

"I shall do as I can," replied Carina.

And the meal continued.

"It is strange that a man does not wish to eat and share with his clan," said Nalon, hoping not to overstep the bonds of friendship thus far attained.

"He is always missing from meals," said Dorak. "But tonight he should not be gone."

"Why is that?" asked Nalon.

"Tonight there is a full moon," replied the chief, "and always on a full moon one of our young men goes missing."

"Which is why Warrigal would not care," interrupted Tuart [a type of eucalypt], the clan wirinum. "For he is old; some say too old for this world and too old for the next. He has lived many long years and seen many changes."

"You would think that an old man with such a beautiful young wife would look forward to be attended to."

"Carina," said Dorak. "Please tell us, what is it that your husband does by himself at night?"

"I cannot answer for him," replied Carina. "You shall have to ask him yourself."

"And when does he eat if not with us?" queried Tuart.

"I cannot answer for him," replied Carina. "You shall have to ask him yourself."

"Is he not satisfied with you," pushed Dorak of the issue, "one so young and beautiful."

"I cannot answer for him," replied Carina. "You shall have to ask him yourself."

Dorak turned to Nalon. "We have not seen him for some time now. It would reflect badly upon us if he should pass from this world due to our combined inability as a clan to help secure his old age."

"It is wonderful that you should consider him," said Nalon. "But if he refuses aid from his wife then I see no reason why you should accept any dishonour. You have done more than a good chief should do. You have imparted good judgement by acquiring about him, and on the other hand you do not part poor judgement upon his wife for refusing to offer good cause."

"Maybe I am too young to be a chief," said Dorak, "too inexperienced."

"I wish all the chiefs of the land were as young as you," replied Nalon, and Dorak understood his meaning.

The following morning there was much gasping, much talk, but banter, but most of all there was great concern from the parents of the young man missing.

Nalon stood before Kalti and explained what he had learnt.

"A young man has disappeared in the middle of the night," said Nalon. "They say we might have something to do with it but most consider it the usual, for men always go missing on the night of the full moon."

"What manner of a beast takes a young man at full moon?" asked Kalti.

"You think him dead," said Nalon.

"From all I have heard I consider him eaten," replied Kalti. "But I also heard a strange noise last night."

"Yes," said Nalon. "I heard it too."

"And someone investigated," continue Kalti, "and then I fell back to sleep."

Nalon was then struck with a consideration of the issue, one that pointed to drastic action being taken, for if Death was involved then he needed to find out.

"I shall go to the chief and have word with him," said Nalon.

"And I shall come with you."

When Nalon saw the chief he also noticed that the wirinum was with him. Kalti and Nalon approached.

"I hope we are not intruding," said Nalon, "but we heard, and were concerned, by the disappearance of another young man."

"Yes, this is true," said Dorak. "It is a terrible thing and we do not know what to do about it."

"I am only new here," said Nalon, "and know little of matters concerning your clan, but with all I have witnessed I have drawn simple conclusion."

"Please, tell me," urged Dorak.

"It might be a matter of internal insecurities where the one named Warrigal has seen to the demise of the young men within this small community."

"He is but an old man," insisted Tuart, the wirinum. "How could he have anything to do with this thing of misfortune?"

"Warrigal is never seen, in particular at night. His humpy is far enough from here, that you cannot see, nor smell, what occurs in his midst; and he burns his own fire. His wife has little to do with him and appears estranged towards him. Young men go missing during a full moon, which would provide anyone enough light by night to cause great mischief upon another. A young man would sooner face his fear of the night than wake another, showing even the slightest cowardice, and therefore attempts to forage through the night to lay investigation upon any mysterious sound which might penetrate his young ear. I fear the worse for the young man but believe your answers might lay with Warrigal and his humpy."

"I think you are right," agreed Dorak. "We must investigate, immediately."

Not before too long the chief had together a small group of ten men with three spears each, not including Dorak and Tuart who only carried one apiece. They then moved though the bush and towards the humpy of Warrigal.

Having seen the group of men moving out towards the humpy belonging to her husband, Carina took up a tomahawk and filed in behind them, but some distance from them so not to be seen.

It did not take long before the men fell upon the humpy and immediately everything fell into place.

Warrigal was sitting there with his back towards them. He was making so much noise that he did not hear their approach. He was gnawing on the cooked but fleshy leg of his victim from the night before, eating man-flesh as though it was goanna, possum, or beast.

"What is the meaning of this!" voiced Dorak.

Warrigal stood up and swung around, stooped slightly in his old age. "I... I was hungry. My wife has failed to bring me food."

Suddenly, Carina leapt from hiding and said: "This is not true. You are a monster."

"And there is only one way in which to treat such a monster," said Dorak, and without further word, but by the simply hand signal given to the group, Warrigal was struck down.

Warrigal cowered, hunched over and then fell to the ground. He was on all fours and then fell to his belly as his arms and legs were severely disfigured. The group then flung their spears at the old man Warrigal until not a single spear was left to throw, but the old man was still alive.

Dorak was about to move forward and finish him off when Nalon intervened.

"It is enough that his arms and legs are disfigured, and that his body is riddled with spears," said Nalon. "Let him go; let him wonder off as best he can into the bush. He has eaten man-flesh, and this is a very bad thing to do. I have made errors during my time on walkabout. The Madhi are now dingoes, but should not be afforded respect, and so to eat the meat of a dingo is not unkind or against the law, and so it shall not be against the law to hunt and kill for food this creature that I shall now create."

And before their very eyes the old man Warrigal was turned into an echidna, the spears turned to spines upon his back.

"Warrigal has eaten man-flesh and so we, all that is the creation of Baiame, shall be rewarded with eating the meat of the echidna. This is not against the law. Let him go now and procreate."

And without further word Nalon turned away from the escaping Warrigal now a creature which would spend eternity searching for ants and termites, for he could eat nothing else, his mouth having shrivelled to such a degree that he could not open it wide enough to gnaw upon the bones of men.

Nalon then lifted his eyes for he saw Carina standing there before him. She looked as though struck with horror. She withdrew her tomahawk from behind her back and savagely beat herself, repeatedly, in the head. Blood gushed down her face and upon her chest, covering her entire front in red.

Nalon lifted his hands in command and said: "The beautiful Carina does not deserve such punishment and self-mutilation and so I command it that she be spared humility. From this day fourth she shall become a robin, to fly high, take to the sky, and to eat the insects of this world and be seen for the beauty that she beholds. Let her sing to the world."

When next the group of men blinked and looked upon her form she was a beautiful bird with red breast. Carina unfolded her wings for the first time and took to the sky, singing beautifully and she ascended, to forever more offer the world beautiful sight and sound.

Dorak approached Nalon and thanked him. What Nalon had done this night was more than any other had achieved over the past year.

"And what shall you do now, Nalon; or should I call you Baiame?" asked the chief.

"I cannot admit, by any degree, that I should be worthy of such stature," said Nalon, "but my intention is to continue with my task, for there is much to do."

"I think you are Baiame," said Dorak. "I do not believe you are an old man any more than I believe your name is Nalon. I think you are truly the creator of all the good things in life that we see and hear."

"If you are happy and content to believe that I am Baiame then I am Baiame," agreed Nalon, for he knew that the Great Father Spirit would not mind it in the least.

Nalon turned to Kalti.

"Come, Kalti; for we must be getting along. Our work here has been done and further awaits us in the journey ahead."

And without further ado or word the two men departed the good company of the Manilla clan.

WAHN, THE MIMIC

Wahn stood on the edge of the clearing to the camp, his chief standing before him and handing over the last of what were to be his possessions.

This was the Coreen [the end of the hills] clan and they had had enough of Wahn and his laziness.

"You must go now," said Nardu [a plant with edible seeds], the chief. "Do not come back for we have had enough of your laziness. You are making the women as lazy as you for you entice them so easily with the way in which you take but do not give. Take those things I have given you; a dilly-bag with a little food, a firestick, kangaroo bone and rope made of hair. You have your spear and throwing stick which are your own."

"If you send me away," said Wahn, with a sad but angry heart, "then you will regret it."

"Do not play games with me, Wahn," said Nardu. "Your time here is up."

Nardu turned his back on Wahn and walked back into the clearing where the remainder of the clan rested. Wahn could do little more than turn slowly and walk away into the thickness of the bush which surrounded him: though a short walk to the south would see the world revealed as it opened up into the plains of roaming beasts.

Wahn continued on but did not go further than a half days journey; in fact he went just far enough that he could still see the camp fires burning at the Coreen clan after the sun dipped away, the cicadas and other insects enjoying the night.

Wahn considered his revenge and considered it well. Immediately he set about making a small camp of his own, a camp with a big fire and five good shelters [shelters are called miamia or mia-mia (gunyah, humpy, wurley, lean-to or vaulted hut are other names of others types of shelters and huts)].

The following day Wahn scrambled up the nearest tall tree and prepared a lookout, from which he could monitor the coming and going of persons within the camp of the Coreen clan. This satisfied him and his plan. That night he perched himself here and waited the return of the hunting group that had gone in search of game earlier that morning. It was then that his insight gave vestige of surety for another reason, for a man of another nearby clan had wondered behind the others and had taken the route that offered danger but speed: which happened to be close to his camp.

Wahn quickly climbed down the tree and moved into one of the huts and let his skills perform their magic. He mimicked a crying baby; a small group of individuals; the sound of someone chopping word; and finally, the most magic of all, a singing woman with such a lovely sound that a man could fall in love quite easily without even setting eyes upon her.

The lone hunter came upon the camp and saw Wahn.

"Ah, I knew I heard something. What is your name?" asked Nambur [a tea-tree].

"My name is Wahn," replied Wahn.

"I thought I heard someone singing."

"No, there is no one here," said Wahn, eyeing the small kyeema that Nambur had over his shoulder. "Your load looks heavy. Place it down and rest; I do not mind if you do."

"No; no tricks now," said Nambur, ignoring Wahn and his offer. "I know I heard voices, and a beautiful voice, too." He looked left and right, squinting in the light of the fire. "There are many miamia here. Where is everyone? This must be a new camp. It smells new. I never knew a camp existed so close to the Coreen."

"These huts are empty," said Wahn. "As to the voice, I know not of what you speak. There is no one here but me. I have made these miamia so that weary travellers may rest. You look weary, Nambur. Maybe you are so tired that you are hearing voices."

"Yes, maybe you are right," agreed Nambur as he placed the small kyeema upon the ground.

"Where are you from?" asked Wahn.

"I am from the Arika [a waterlily] clan."

"Well, that is some distance yet. Why don't you just rest here for the night; I do not mind if you do."

"I must get back or else the kyeema meat will spoil."

"You can cook it here," said Wahn. "I shall help you. You can then rest till morning and the meat will not be spoiled."

"Yes, I suppose you are right," and having said that, Nambur turned to the fire and held his palms up to it, to feel the warmth.

Now, with his back towards Wahn, Wahn rushed up and pushed poor Nambur into the fire which engulfed him. Wahn picked up his spear and shuffled the coals around quickly in order for Nambur to become completely covered in coals so that his body would feed the fire and burn away, all evidence of his existence disappearing from the world. Wahn then sat back leisurely as he cooked the kyeema for himself.

Wahn continued with his tricks, mimics, and enticements for seven days and on the eighth day one of the chiefs of a nearby clan posed a question in the hope that someone could give an answer.

"Where is the hunter, Yuka [a tree]?" asked chief Mowan [the sun] of the Arora [a cockatoo] clan."

"He has not returned from the previous night," said a voice.

"And I heard that several other clans, also, are missing men," said another.

Arora turned then to a messenger. "Go and see the chief of the nearby clans, see if they are missing any hunters, for I find this thing very strange."

And so the messenger went about his task and returned the following day, having bypassed the miamias where Wahn sat lonely.

Again he chief addressed the clan. "Men have gone missing from all about," said Mowan. "We must investigate."

"Maybe it was the bunyip," said one.

"Maybe they simply lost their way," said another.

"No, no; you are all wrong," said a third. "For bunyips live in swamps and hunters do not get lost."

"What is to be done then?" asked Mowan. Something must be done."

It was then that Nalon stepped into the clearing with Kalti at his side. "What is to be done about what?" asked Nalon.

"Who are you?" asked Mowan.

"I am Baiame, and this is my accomplice, Kalti," said Nalon.

Everyone around saw that Nalon was speaking the truth for there was something about him that did not lie.

"What shall we do, Baiame; for we do not know what to do or where to look?" uttered Mowan. "Our men are missing, from all the clans around."

"I have heard similar stories from a group of hunters not far from here," said Baiame. "Men go missing from the area at night; I shall therefore search the ground between the clans when the sun goes down tonight and find you the answers to your questions. Kalti will stay here for he has much to pass on to you in regards to the laws of the land. For your attentiveness I shall bring security to all."

"Thank you, Baiame," voiced Mowan. "But you must look like a hunter. Here, take this," and the chief picked up a recently killed possum. "Carry this upon your shoulder and you will look like one of us, for the way you are at the moment you look as though you have transcended sky-world."

"Thank you," said Baiame, and he walked off into the bush, to wait the fall of night.

It was then that Mowan turned to a hunter, who was always grumpy and a bully, and requested something of him.

"Mulyan," directed the chief. "I want you to follow Baiame from a distance and see what happens. You can report to me once done."

"Yes, Mowan," replied Mulyan as he disappeared into the bush but not close enough to be discovered by Nalon.

Nalon commenced walking soon after dark, traipsing along here and there between all the clans territory that had lost hunters over the past seven days. It was then that he saw a sparkle of light from a fire and heard voices. He heard a bay cry; the chopping of wood; and many other things. And then all of a sudden the most beautiful voice he had ever heard sang out for him to hear.

Immediately Nalon went to investigate.

Nalon stepped out before the five miamia and saw the fire burning.

"Hello," said Nalon. "Is there anyone about?"

Wahn came out of one of the miamia. "Oh, hello; my name is Wahn."

"My name is Uwan [to meet]," lied Nalon. "I heard a beautiful voice and a baby crying; and other sounds too, but... where is everyone?"

"Oh no, you must be mistaken," said Wahn, "for there is no one here but me."

"Oh, well," said Nalon. "Maybe I am simply over-tired. May I sleep here the night?"

"Oh course," said Wahn. "Please, put your possum down and make yourself warm by my fire."

"Thank you," said Nalon, and he put his possum down and turned to face the fire.

It was then that Wahn came up behind Nalon and rushed him, to give him an almighty push, but Nalon moved out of the way at the last moment and Wahn went falling into the fire. He screamed and fought but the fire had a temperament of its own and engulfed him whole.

The body of Wahn was burning furiously and turning to white ash when suddenly Nalon gave a clap of his hands and the ash turned into a white bird which took to a nearby branch in the nearest tree. Instantly Wahn knew that he had been deceived and that Uwan was really Baiame.

"You are evil," said Nalon, "and so I have turned you into a white crow. Everyone will know who you are and will avoid you always, for there are no white crows of this world. You are the first created and shall be the last for I will not create another. There will be no female to keep you company. You shall live eternity a lonely creature and eat the insects of this world in order to help pay your debt to all those you have hurt with your evil ways. Fly now and do not come back."

Wahn said not a word and flew off into the night as Nalon made his way back to Mowan and Kalti to report on the disappearance of the hunters. After he had gone Mulyan came out of hiding with a smile upon his face and rubbed his hands together.

"Now I can go to the Coreen and bully Nardu into giving me the sister of Wahn as a bride, for she is beautiful."

WAHN THE WHITE CROW

Wahn was rather upset by the fact that he had been discovered and by Baiame at that. Being malcontent with this small fact he leapt from branch to branch and tree to tree to see what mischief he could cause but it soon come about that there was little he could do other than mimic a few old favourite sounds, though in his present form these abilities were fading, fast.

Nalon had returned to the camp and explained all to the chief there and along with Kalti continued into the next day, walking slowly through the bush until they fell upon the Coreen.

"This must be the Coreen," said Kalti. "Mowan told me about them. There is a good relationship between the two clans, except for one particular hunter named Mulyan, of the Arora."

"Who is Mulyan?" asked Nalon.

"One of the most hated men in the region, and he likes to have his own way."

After giving introduction to several people of the Coreen, who were not that concerned to see Nalon and Kalti approach, they were pointed in the right direction with the purse of the lips and immediately approached the miamia where Mowan resided.

Nalon called out to Mowan when he stepped up to the front of the miamia.

"Chief Mowan," called Nalon. "Are you in there?"

"Yes, I am here," said Mowan as he stepped out of his miamia and stood up before Nalon. "I am chief Mowan. Who are you and what can I do for you?"

"I am Baiame, and this is Kalti," said Nalon.

The jaw of the chief dropped as he heard the name and realised immediately that it must be true for the mam before him had not been struck down dead.

"I have news of the hunters that have gone missing, and of the recent disappearance of one from Arora."

"Ah, we heard," said Mowan.

"How did you hear?" asked Nalon.

"Well, you see," began Mowan, "the hunter named Mulyan came here just last night and requested the hand of the sister of Wahn. No one dare get in his way, and as she had no one else to support her... well, I gave my blessing... just to be rid of him more than anything else, you understand of course."

"Of course," said Nalon. "I am Baiame, I understand everything," and a vision suddenly fell upon him. He saw the place within the mountains that Mulyan had taken the beautiful young girl.

And so the conversation continued for a little while before Nalon and Kalti settled down in the empty miamia made vacant by the new bride.

The following morning, after Nalon had exhausted himself with lecture upon the chief, trying with all his effort to have him abide by the laws of the land, a few murmurs sprang to ear.

Nalon exit his miamia and looked on as the man named Mulyan stepped past him with a grimace upon his face. To Nalon he looked as though he was up to no good.

Mulyan walked, quite purposely, up to a woman and snatched her digging stick from right within her hands, the smoke of her fire filling her eyes with tears.

"Hey, that digging stick is mine," cried the middle-aged woman. "Give it back. It is not yours." It was then that the smoke cleared and she saw who it was. "Oh, it is you, Mulyan. I would be glad for you to borrow it for a while."

"I may wish keep it," said Mulyan.

"Please, feel free," said the woman. "It is time I got myself another, anyway. We become too attached to these things, sometimes."

Mulyan stormed off and back into the bush and as he passed another fire he tore a piece of flesh from a possum and took it with himself.

At that instant, Kalti came out of the miamia. "What was that all about?"

"I do not know," said Nalon. "Sometimes these things are clouded. It is always the way where some amount of evil is lurking in the corner."

"You must be clouded most of the time, then," said Kalti. "For most people me meet have some form of malign intent hidden within them."

"This is true," agreed Nalon. "But nevertheless, I think we should watch him carefully, for I fear that he might have done his new wife an injustice."

They followed Mulyan until he came to a tree. Mulyan looked up, and Nalon and Kalti followed his gaze. Up there in the tree they saw Wahn, fast asleep upon the upper most of the branches.

"It appears that Mulyan has been spying upon us," whispered Nalon, "for he knows Wahn is a white crow."

"As we are spying upon him, no doubt," said Kalti.

They continued to watch as Mulyan dug a deep hole and then placed the meat into it. He then made a covering for the hole made of crossed sticks and wove into the cross sections some grass and others small vines. Mulyan then took some cordage he had made of intestines, which he carried tied around his waist, and connected one end to the trap and the other over the nearest branch. He then hid behind the tree trunk and pulled on the cordage so that the roof of the trap was lifted into the air until it disappeared from view in the leaves overhead.

Mulyan now sat and waited but he did not have to wait long.

Wahn woke up and sniffed the air. He could smell freshly cooked meat. Mm, freshly cooked meat was better than digging for worms.

Wahn flew down to the edge of the trap and looked into it. It was easy to see it was a trap but he considered it. If he flew into the trap quick enough he was sure to be able to fly out soon enough, and with the hunger for fresh meat eating at him he flew down into the hole immediately.

Suddenly the roof fell down from the branches and onto the trap, covering the hole. Wahn quickly grabbed the meat and flew up, hitting his head on the roof. At this same moment, Mulyan stepped out from hiding with the digging stick and very briskly moved over to the trap.

"Let me out," ordered a frightened Wahn. "Whoever has imprisoned me here please let me out."

"It is I, Mulyan. I have taken your sister away from her home and you shall never see her again."

Mulyan suddenly removed the cover to the trap and hit Wahn over the head with the digging stick.

Wahn fell to the bottom of the trap and was semi-conscious when Mulyan started filling the hole back in again with the digging stick he had taken as his own.

Mulyan was concentrating so hard upon the digging that he did not notice Wahn wake and commence with his escape, by digging himself a small concave at the bottom of the hole and pushing his body into it.

Once the hole was filled Mulyan looked rather content. He flung the digging stick away into the bush and walked away back to his home in the mountains.

Nalon and Kalti came out of hiding.

"What shall we do?" asked Kalti.

"It is only Wahn," said Nalon. "But I fear for his sister and so we shall follow Mulyan and see what we find."

They followed Mulyan all the way to his miamia which was situated upon a small knoll leading up to the mountains. By the time Nalon and Kalti saw it they were exhausted, but not exhausted enough to see what Mulyan had been up to.

Mulyan had disliked Wahn so much that he had taken his sister into his shelter, had his way with her and then set her to work. She was dragging in a large kyeema from the bottom of the mountain.

"Have you not yet got that up here?" demanded Mulyan. "I want it cooked and ready by tonight, for I am very hungry. When you are finished cooking it you can prepare its skin as a blanket for me, for I grow very cold by night. Keep the fire burning and get some more firewood, fill the bladders up with water, and hurry up about you."

"It would seem that she is tending to him," said Kalti.

"Yes," agreed Nalon. "And look yonder, and see what I see."

Nalon pointed with his lips and Kalti saw. Wahn had just landed in a tree. He had dug himself another hole out of the one he had been trapped in, by digging himself upwards from the concave shelter he had created and pushing the dirt behind him as he advance upwards to freedom.

"He is a courageous bird," said Nalon, "but a very lazy man."

They both watched Wahn, and Wahn watched Mulyan, and Mulyan worked his wife hard.

Later that night Mulyan turned to his wife, who was nothing more to him than a concubine and slave. "I shall be gone a short time," he said. "Stay here and keep the fire burning, for I seek some female companionship below the mountain; companionship which you cannot offer, but I am free to take."

Mulyan departed and moved down the sloping ground, but Wahn saw him leave and took to the sky, darting off before him. Nalon and Kalti followed, quietly.

Wahn recognised the general direction in which Mulyan was walking and headed that way immediately. It was his own old haunt, the miamias he had used to capture the poor hunters that came his way in order for him to take their food.

Once at the miamias he perched himself upon a branch. He saw a torch light in the distance. It could only be the one that was seeking to appease Mulyan. Mulyan had, no doubt, bullied someone into providing for his needs. He looked in the other direction and saw that Mulyan was even closer than before.

"Now I shall get a small portion of revenge upon this Mulyan," said Wahn and made out to be a beautiful female, mimicking the voice to the best of his ability.

Mulyan heard the voice and called out, but not loud enough for the real woman, who was still some distance away, to hear. "I am coming," said Mulyan. "I hope you have brought food with you."

Wahn smiled to himself and then felt silly; for he had no idea what he was going to do to Mulyan once he appeared before him.

"I hear you, my sweet," said Mulyan, grimacing. "I hunger for your flesh and your food."

Mulyan fell upon the camp and looked around. There was no one to be seen.

"Where are you?" called Mulyan, softly. "Come out this instant or I shall see to it that your husband is killed when next I go hunting."

So that is it, thought Nalon. Mulyan is misusing a wife and threatening the life of another. If there was evil in the world then he had found it.

Wahn was suddenly filled with outrage and flung himself down towards the waiting Mulyan and at the same instant Nalon could take no more and clapped his hands, and as he did so a lightning bolt struck Mulyan into millions of cinders which puffed up in the air and started to drift to the ground.

Wahn was most shocked, the sparks of the lightening covering him from head to tip of tail, and as the dust cleared away Wahn could do nothing but look himself up and down to make sure he was whole. And he was, but he was now a smoky-white crow, a dull grey colour brought on by the lightening. It was then that he got another start and saw Nalon step from the bush with Kalti by his side.

Nalon looked at Wahn with a half-smile and clapped his hands one more time and from the ashes and cinders, laying there upon the ground, up flew Mulyan, for he had now been turned into an eaglehawk.

Nalon looked at Kalti. "Our job is done here." And to Wahn he said this. "Till next time we meet I hope you shall commit further honest labour."

THE REVENGE OF WAHN

For several days Wahn had been watching Mulyan. Mulyan had found himself a nice little nest; one obviously stolen from another bird for Wahn could see the remains of a decaying body at the base of the large gum tree.

Wahn started to creep forward towards the base of this tree in order to see if he knew the bird that Mulyan had killed, for it did not rest well with him that the eaglehawk should be killing others, though this is exactly what he had been doing not so long ago. Maybe it was the mistreatment and disappearance of his sister that had changed the way in which he thought.

Suddenly Mulyan heard something and looked down from there within the comfort of his nest.

"Who is that?" he screamed. "Why, it is Wahn. What are you doing, Wahn? You look very suspicious from up here."

"I have come to see the dead bird," said Wahn. "The way in which you have dispensed with it and taken its nest is very cunning and shrewd. I like the way you do things, Mulyan. I am just seeking the knowledge you have on such undertakings. Will you teach me your cunning ways for we are now both birds, even if of a different feather?"

"No; go away," replied Mulyan. "If I were to give my secrets out to every bird that came along then they wouldn't be secrets any longer, and before you knew it I would be without a home. Besides, I am going soon, to look for food."

"May I come along?" asked Wahn. "I would be extremely interested and very appreciative."

"You could not keep up with me, Wahn," laughed Mulyan. "I am not messing around simply in order for you to get a few pointers on how to hunt."

"I shall keep up with you as best I can," pleaded Wahn. "I promise."

"Oh; very well; so long as you can keep up with me I shall do all I can to show you what is to be done in order to be as cunning as I."

And so Mulyan leapt into the sky and was off with Wahn close behind him.

They had not been flying long when Mulyan pointed something out to Wahn.

"Look down there, Wahn, and you shall see a nest belonging to a family of bush rats," said Mulyan.

"I do not see anything," said Wahn.

"That is because your eyes are no good, Wahn," scoffed Mulyan. "This is why I will always get the better of you in the hunt. Come down now and I shall show you a thing or two."

They both flew down and Wahn was quick to perch himself upon a branch as Mulyan went about his duty of getting something to eat.

"Please leave something for me to chew on," pleaded Wahn, "for I am very hungry."

"I shall leave you what I can," said Mulyan, "but not before I have eaten everything that I can of the inhabitants of that nest."

Wahn watched carefully as Mulyan jumped up and down to squash the grass within the nest and tore apart all the little rats within that he found. As Mulyan was busy with this, and eating what he had killed, Wahn took a pointed kangaroo bone which he had hidden in his wing and placed in upright in another nest nearby, but this nest was empty. He then pulled at the grass around it with his beak so that the pointed kangaroo bone could not been seen with the naked eye. Wahn then flew back up to the branch on which he was previously perched.

"You are doing a good job, Mulyan," congratulated Wahn of his efforts. "Is there anything left for me?"

Mulyan swallowed the last mouthful that he could possibly cram in. "I think I have finished. Here, you can have this little one; a newborn."

"Oh, thank you, Mulyan," cried Wahn as he leapt from his branch and landed upon the carcass that Mulyan had left for him.

"Now I have shown you a thing or two," said Mulyan, "so maybe you will be so kind as to leave me alone."

And with that said Mulyan flew away back to his nest in the gum tree.

The following day, just as the sun was rising over the horizon, Wahn landed with a heavy thud on the branch next to Mulyan.

"Quickly, Mulyan," said Wahn, pretending to be exhausted and tired all at the same time. "I have found another nest of rats for you to sup upon."

"What?" screamed Mulyan, more surprised than not. "Where is this nest?"

"It is very close to the other one you invaded yesterday," said Wahn.

"Oh no, I know that nest. It is empty, I assure you," said Mulyan without a doubt in his mind.

"No, there are rats in it, for I saw them with my own eyes," said Wahn.

"So why did you not eat them yourself?" asked Mulyan.

"The nest is full of grass and the rats are hiding within," said Wahn. "The grass is too long and thick for me to squash down, but an eaglehawk of your calibre would have no trouble at all. All you need to do is hop and jump around as you did yesterday and those rats will be ours," continued Wahn. "But you can have the first pick and I shall just take what is left."

"Well, thank you, Wahn," said Mulyan. "It would seem that you are finally coming of your senses."

Wahn lead the way to the nest, although Mulyan knew the way, and once there Wahn returned to his earlier perching station and watched as Mulyan landed upon the empty next with a heavy thud and jumped around to squash the grass.

"Argh," screamed Mulyan.

"What is it?" shouted Wahn. "What is wrong? Are you alright?"

"No, I am not," returned Mulyan. "There is a kangaroo bone in here which has been sharpened to a point. I have been injured and now I cannot walk or fly as efficiently as I could before."

"Oh, you poor thing," said Wahn, upset that Mulyan did not die. "Can you make it back to your nest?"

"No, I do not think so," said Mulyan. "I think I can just make it to the other rat nest, the one we cleared out yesterday, for I am not staying in this one. It would kill me if I rolled upon the bone in my sleep."

And so Mulyan took almost all day to move himself into the other empty nest and then fell asleep, exhausted.

Later that night, when the moon was full, Mulyan woke up from his slumber for he had heard a noise.

He opened his eyes and saw Wahn at the other nest, for his eyesight was very good.

Wahn was careful to take the kangaroo bone from the nest and then tucked it away within his wing, a wide smile upon his face. Wahn then leapt into the night sky, found another nearby nest, and planted it again as he had the day before.

Mulyan pondered on this and knew straight away what was going on. He had been tricked by Wahn.

"I see you, Wahn!" screamed Mulyan. "So, it was you that planted that kangaroo bone."

Wahn looked up, half shocked. "Yes, it was I," admitted Wahn. "And I only wish that it had killed you the first time, for I would not allow such a mistake to happen a second time."

"I will kill you myself, now, Wahn!" threatened Mulyan.

Without further ado Wahn leapt off into the night and disappeared from sight.

The next day Mulyan was feeling much better and decided to go hunting for Wahn. It was not long before he came upon a robin.

"If you tell me what I want to know then I shall not kill you, Robin," said Mulyan.

The robin was clearly frightened half to death. "W... w... what is it you want to know?"

"Have you see Wahn around here?" asked Mulyan. "He looks like a grey crow; a dirty looking bird."

"Oh, y... yes, I have," said Robin. "He went that way, towards a small cave upon that rise."

"Good," said Mulyan. "Now go, before I change my mind and decide to eat you."

The robin flew away posthaste and Mulyan continued on and soon fell upon the cave entrance as indicated by the robin.

"Come out, Wahn," said Mulyan quite deliberately. "I know you are in there."

"Then come in and get me," said Wahn.

"Oh, no," said Mulyan, as a matter of fact. "I will not fall for any more of your tricks."

Mulyan then spent the remainder of the morning gathering wood and found the camp fire of a nearby clan and withdrew a burning stick from within.

Mulyan next lit the wood pile he had created at the front of the cave.

"Your time is up now, Wahn, for the smoke will force you out and then I shall attack and kill you."

"I shall not come out," said Wahn.

"Then you shall die," finished Mulyan of his deliberation.

The fire raged and smoke billowed out and into the mouth of the cave. Mulyan smiled as he watched. It would not be long now and Wahn would come wobbling out, lungs filled with smoke.

Several minutes later and Mulyan heard a voice, loud and clear.

"This is nice weather we are having here," said Wahn.

Mulyan looked up and could not believe his eyes. Wahn was standing upon a rock at the top of the cave entrance.

"How did you get out?" asked Mulyan, extremely infuriated.

"I had an escape plan," said Wahn. "A chimney existed to the rear of my cave."

"Hah; and look what it did to you," shouted Mulyan in laughter. "You are now dark brown all over because of the smoke; almost black. You look dirtier than ever. All the animals will be laughing at you now, Wahn." And Mulyan bent over in laughter.

Wahn looked down upon himself and was overcome with hatred for Mulyan. He did look rather dirty. And not to miss an opportunity, Wahn quickly flew away as fast as he could, knowing full well that Mulyan would have trouble keeping up with him, his wing undoubtedly not quite fully recovered.

Mulyan simply stood there laughing, walking around in hysterics, hobbling about due to his injury caused by the kangaroo bone.

THE BLACK CROW

Wahn continued on his own, having adventures no matter where he travelled, and as he grew in age his feathers changed colour until one day he woke and found that he was now entirely black: a black crow. And on and on his life continued.

He pondered upon his existence and then he pondered on his adventures as a black crow, as he remembered them.

He recalled how he had encountered an unknown hunter. The hunter had a firestick but it had burnt out and Wahn showed him how to make fire by taking a stick with a point and then rolling it in the palms of his hands, the point of the stick drilling a hole in hardwood until it was so hot that it gave off smoke. By adding dry grass a fire had started. With this the hunter never went cold and also used fire to burn large areas of grassy plain in order to direct animals into his traps. There was another time when he wished to deceive the pelicans by seeing to it that the babies were placed into a nest high above the ground. The pelicans, on their return, were going to kill Wahn for his horrible act but realised that in doing so Wahn had saved their lives, for the wonambi could not reach them. The pelicans ended up thanking Wahn for his trouble. In another instance there were many animals such as the tortoise, frogs, and lizards, all insect eaters and the creation of Baiame, who had been helped by Wahn in finding their diverse paths into the future and casting a history upon their ancestral heritage, each species being defined in their own way, each turning to having relations with their totem ancestors which was far more diverse than the totem ancestors of men and women who could not have sexual relations due to clan laws forbidding incest. And his most effortless good deed was when he discovered a flock of black crows, just like him, who he commanded to give aid to several naked swans that were freezing to death. By shaking their wings the crows dislodged many feathers which then encased the swans and saved them from misery and death, which is why there are black swans as well as white ones.

Where had the black crows come from, for he had never seen them before that day, and they soon disappeared after the good deed was performed: Wahn was too old to keep up with them as they flew away.

Then, one day, as the sky began to turn dark with the coming of night, Wahn had stumbled carelessly upon a camp fire, and who should be there but Baiame and Kalti.

"Ah, Wahn," said Nalon with a smile. "I am happy to see you here."

"Why, Baiame," started Wahn, "what horrors are you going to delivery upon me this day?"

"No bad delivery," said Nalon. "I should hope."

"Do not keep me in suspense, please," pleaded Wahn. "Do what you will to me and I shall be on my way. I did not mean to stumble upon your fire."

"Wahn," said Nalon in a friendly manner. "I have heard of all the good things you have been doing. The blacker you turn, the more good you do: but now I see you are the blackest. You have been ostracized by everyone you meet but you have learnt to do good instead of evil. I am going to reward you."

"What... you mean, nothing bad is to happen to me?" said Wahn, excited by the words of Baiame.

"I shall give you a gift," said Nalon. "What shall it be?"

Wahn considered this carefully. "Firstly I wish to know what that flock of black birds were."

"I have turned a clan into crows, in the hope that they shall follow your path and do good as you have done."

"Well, in that case I shall like to make a request," started Wahn. "I wish to be white once more, never to be black again, but further more I wish to be able to look down upon the land you have created and see all the mischief that is created."

"Do I understand you correctly?" asked Nalon. "Do you wish to be a star, to be alight in the sky at night, to forever be witness to the goings on upon this land?"

"Yes, that is it," said an excited Wahn. "I wish to be a star."

And with a clap of his hands Nalon did turn Wahn into a star and cast him high above the land so that he could watch all the mischief that others got up to, forever to sit high in the sky, winking and blinking, and laughing away at the acts of others.

No sooner had Wahn been turned into a star and the crows upon the land started to make a raucous. They saw Wahn had been turned into a star and even to this day can still be seen flying around in the sky calling out his name for all to hear: "Wahn, Wahn, Wahn."

OLBA AND PANGARI

Nalon and Kalti had found themselves in very good company. The clan was the Ngadjuri and they were renowned for their exceptional hunters; namely two men who were Kudnu and Wulkinara.

Nalon and Kalti, as with most of the clan, had just finished with the main meal of the day when a man came screaming into the clearing, looking frantically for the whereabouts of the chief of the clan, who was known as Killara [permanent, always there].

"Killara, Killara, it has happened again," screamed the hunter.

Everyone around, excluding Nalon and Kalti, all knowinf instantly what the matter was. Everyone stood up and started to fear the worse, talking amongst themselves, fearing for their lives.

"Calm down," ordered Killara. "Tell us what has happened."

And as he told his story the people of the Ngadjuri commenced to pack up their things, ready and very eager to move along.

"We were returning when we fell upon a known track," started the warrior to the open gasps of those that knew, which was all those within earshot. "We tried to skirt around but were suddenly surrounded by the old woman and her two dogs." [These two dogs are actually a thylacoleo (marsupial lion) which are slightly larger than a hyena. They are ferocious meat-eaters. They have huge claws and slicing teeth, weigh approximately 100kg, are 1.5m in length, and can easily bring down the monster mallee-akana – diprotodon. They ambush their prey and chase it down].

The chief looked on beyond where the warrior stood and knew none others had survived. And the warrior continued. "The others have been torn from limb to limb and none have survived."

The clan had started to move away, the chief was bewildered and stood up, ready to join them. Nalon and Kalti stood too, but only as a courtesy for they felt little fear, in particular as they did not fully understand the situation.

"The old woman and her dogs have returned," voiced the chief for all to hear as they began the retreat. "We must vacate this camp and never return."

"Wait! All of you! Stop!" yelled Kudnu. "Where are you all going to?"

Wulkinara stood up beside him. "Listen, all of you. You cannot give up your land like this. We must stay and fight."

"She is too strong for us, and those dogs of hers are monsters," reminded one. "They have death written all over them."

Nalon looked at Kalti and Kalti returned the glare. Death had something to do with this. This was the doings of Yowie.

"She is but an old woman. Are you afraid of an old woman?" challenged Kudnu.

"She has sharp, pointed teeth, just like her dogs. I have seen her myself," advised another. "She ripped the throat out of a man."

"Are you to simply give up your territory to her?" asked Wulkinara, pointlessly.

"If it means saving my life and the life of my family then yes, I will vacate."

"Will none of you stay here and help us defend the camp?" asked Kudnu.

No one answered; they simply walked away leaving Kudnu and Wulkinara alone. Within a very short space of time the entire clan site had been vacated.

Kudnu looked over to Nalon and Kalti as Wulkinara brought over several spears.

"Why are you not joining the throng?" asked Kudnu. "Are you not afraid?"

"To be afraid of dying is one thing, to be afraid of Death is another," replied Nalon, to which Kudnu and Wulkinara did not pick up on the naming of Yowie. "And considering that I am not afraid of either then I guess I have to answer no."

"And what of your friend," indicated Wulkinara, of Kalti.

"I cannot go," said Kalti. "For I must remain with... my friend."

Nalon smiled at this.

"You are braver men, both, than those of this clan," said Kudnu.

"But members no more," added Wulkinara.

"You are too hard on them," said Nalon.

"Who are you to insult me like that?" demanded Wulkinara.

"I shall answer that for you," said Kalti, with a smile. "For he is Baiame."

"Do not fool us with your words," said Wulkinara, "nor breathe such unscrupulous words here. Do not take the name of the creator and soil it."

With not a further word said, Nalon lifted up both his hands and within his palms suddenly appeared two boomerangs.

The two men were aghast at such magic. "What is the meaning of this?"

Explaining such meaning was frivolous to Nalon and he did not have time, so he offered other assistance more meaningful to two hunters the calibre of those before him.

"These are weapons, and they are called boomerang. You can hurl them at a target," Explained Nalon, "and they shall return to you if you should miss, so you can try again as you may until you hit your target. But it is more affective in the open."

Kudnu took one of the weapons and Wulkinara the other.

"These are truly weapons of sky-world," said Kudnu, "for I have never seen such a thing."

"They are a gift to all men as created by Baiame," said Kalti. "This weapon is spreading across the face of the land, from East to West; South and North."

Kudnu weighed it in his hand. "How do I use is?"

"I think you already know," said Nalon as he smiled, "but I shall show you anyway, and by the time the old woman and her two dogs come calling you shall both be ready."

"If you are truly Baiame," started Wulkinara, "then why do you not infer good judgement upon this mad woman and her dogs, to stop them dead in their tracks?"

"For they are the creation of Yowie, and Yowie is death. To infer force upon these three may interrupt the future gains to be awarded us. The less I interfere, the less opportunity Death has of being successful at his game. Only now am I starting to learn this, for as I grow in my own personal knowledge, so Yowie grows in power. The power growth must be put to a stop. You must confront this woman and her two dogs on your own. Do you accept the challenge set before you?"

"Yes," said the two brave men as though a single entity.

Nalon looked up then, into the night sky which had drawn around them. "She will not be here till morning. She has put herself to sleep. You will encounter her on the morrow, after practising with the boomerangs I have given you. By the time the sun is at its highest the old woman will be amongst us. Kalti and I shall watch from a distance and will not interfere."

The following morning the two strong men walked towards the edge of the forest and the plains and there in the distance they saw what they already knew: the old woman and her two dogs had changed direction and approach, as she always did when attacking a camp.

Kalti and Nalon were behind them as the hunters looked at one another before turning to Nalon.

"She very rarely changes her tactics, Baiame," said Kudnu. "She always approaches from the thicket of scrub and then changes her approach to come from the plains. She thinks she fools clans by doing so but we have come to learn of her ways."

"Do you know how she will attack?" asked Kalti.

"Yes," replied Wulkinara. "She will send in the dogs ahead of her and follow up behind; maybe even slightly to the flank, but not by much. The dogs will do most of the killing before she sets foot upon clan soil."

"Kudnu; Wulkinara," said Nalon. "We cannot stay here to witness the fight nor give encouragement nor assistance, so we shall retire to the camp fire. Once the job has been done you can report to us your victory."

The two warriors looked at each other to ponder on the words, for it was the truest indication they had received that there would be a victory and that the victory would belong to them.

"Thank you, Baiame," said Wulkinara as he weighed the boomerangs in his hand and the two visitors turned and moved away. "It is time, Kudnu. I shall help you up into the branches of this tree; they will not see you hiding. When the dogs are close enough you can distract them and I shall come out of hiding and use the boomerangs to kill these heinous creatures. The old woman will follow, even if I have to kill her with my bare hands."

So Wulkinara helped Kudnu into the tree and then hid himself behind another tree, and the three small dots in the distance become bigger and bigger as they closed the gap.

Wulkinara and Kudnu did not have to wait long and before they knew it the dogs, both Olba [red ochre] and Pangari [shadow of the soul], were just metres from the tree in which Kudnu was waiting. The old woman was far enough behind them that she was safe from a throwing spear but close enough to shout commands to her companions.

As the dogs passed the tree, Kudnu drew their attention by howling like a dingo. Olba and Pangari spared no moment at all in delivering themselves to the base of the tree and began to claw their way up the trunk with Kudnu climbing higher.

Wulkinara suddenly came out of hiding and made further howling sounds, and at the same time threw the first of his boomerangs. The boomerang flew true and hit Olba square in the neck, cutting his head clean away from his shoulders. The dog died instantaneously. Pangari faltered at the sight of this but was soon running towards Wulkinara, Kudnu forgotten. Wulkinara tried to get a good grip on the second boomerang but couldn't and as Pangari leapt up to break his neck, Wulkinara grasped the boomerang in both hands and pounded down as hard as he could upon the back of the dog. He pounded again and again, snapping the bones in the back. Pangari, too, was now dead.

It was now that Wulkinara was startled half to death for the old woman, her pointed teeth and snarly grin, looked deep into his eyes as she stalked him and prepared to pounce, to bite down hard upon his neck and kill him for what he had done to her two precious dogs.

The old woman leapt at Wulkinara but at that precise moment in time Kudnu lashed out with his spear from within the tree and the point of it passed right through the back of her neck and out the front.

The old woman was dead.

Kudnu climbed from the tree and retrieved the spear and Wulkinara stepped up beside him. "We shall burn the woman so that there is nothing left of her to see," he said.

"I agree," answered Wulkinara, "and the dogs, too. They should be buried also."

"No," said Nalon as he stepped from the tree line behind them. "You must bury the dogs. The red one, which is Olba, will foul the ground and produce red ochre. The one called Pangari, which is black, will be buried and foul the ground which in turn will produce black clay. Your clan, and all those around, shall then use the red ochre and black clay to paint marks upon your bodies. With these marks upon you, you shall carry out sacred ceremony in remembrance of this victory and all victories to come, victories upon all of the creatures so created by Yowie, for they deserve nothing more than death."

Wulkinara and Kudnu nodded ascent as Nalon and Kalti looked up into the distance and commenced to walk away.

"Where are you going to?" asked Wulkinara.

"We are on walkabout," replied Nalon.

"Will you not celebrate with us?" tried Kudnu.

"No," said Nalon, "for the walkabout is far too important to leave at rest and unattended."

And the distance between the two parties grew.

THE CANNIBAL

Nalon and Kalti were downwind from a single hut. Before the hut sat a woman, very old and long in the tooth. She sat there without stirring and looked over the flames of her fire as though in a trance. She then began to sing to herself in a flat tone.

Prupe is my name,
I am very old,
But with appetite sublime,
Require sweet meat.

I am set to eat flesh,
So prepared for feast,
The essence of man,
Can bear witness to this.

For with child in arms,
I am bound to eat,
The sweet essence of flesh,
Belonging to kin.

I can no longer resist,
For temptation is longing,
Where food is granted,
And for child I am cunning.

Kalti needed no further convincing and whispered to Nalon: "She is a cannibal. I do not like this place; I fear it."

Prupe looked up, bewildered. "Who is that I hear?" she asked of the wind. "Who is it that stalks me from downwind?"

Nalon had his finger against his lips and Kalti obeyed.

"I know you are there, so speak," urged Prupe. "If you are hungry then please come in. I have a warm fire and just need a little meat. Perhaps you have something with you."

Again both Nalon and Kalti said nothing.

The old woman seemed to listen intently but after a few short minutes returned to her song and the warmth of her fire.

Nalon and Kalti drew back and away, before skirting the camp and continuing on their way.

They had not gone far when they fell upon another camp, though this one was a lot larger.

There were not many people around for most were out hunting or gathering roots and berries, but of those that were present was another elderly woman with a young child walking around near the fire. Nalon approached her with Kalti by his side.

"Hello," said Nalon. "I am Baiame and this is Kalti, my companion."

"My name is Koromarange," said the woman, "but I do not believe you are who you say you are. You shall have to prove it to me."

"Should I have to cast magic for everyone I meet in order for me to be believed?"

The woman shrugged her shoulders. "It means nothing to me," said Koromarange. "I have much more important things on my mind at the moment. But presuming you are who you say you are, which would be hard to prove without a show of magic, what is it that you wish of me?"

"We are passing through the area on walkabout and stumbled across a camp with but a solitary woman in it," explained Nalon. "Who is she and why is she alone and not being looked after?"

Koromarange looked at Nalon but did not answer his question, instead she asked her own. "What is a walkabout?"

"It is the way that marks our sacred existence and makes a man of a child, and it replenishes the sacred existence of our laws to full purpose and fruition. It offers a reminder to clans of the laws provided this land. It is a spiritual awakening and way of life."

"It is many things," said Koromarange.

"It is one small thing," corrected Kalti, "but has many significant meanings."

"And why would one, claiming to be Baiame, be on such a journey?" asked Koromarange.

"To reinstate the laws of the land, to see to it that the clans are brought into line, for me to experience life as you experience it. With each passing day I discover something new and recently I discovered something more, for an old woman, by herself in the wilderness, was singing a song of cannibalistic nature."

"Shhh," ushered Koromarange. "Do not speak loudly of her."

"Why?" asked Kalti, most seriously? "Will she hear us?"

"No," replied Koromarange. "But none other than I know of the truth."

"Tell us," commanded Nalon, in such a manner that Koromarange supposed it to be a request.

"She is a cannibal, it is true," said Koromarange in a whisper, "but worse than that, she eats her kin. I have in my care her only surviving granddaughter, for Prupe is my sister and her granddaughter is of her own child, a child who is now dead. Her granddaughter is named Koakangi. I have to watch her day and night to ensure she is not tempted to go near the old woman, for she misses her grandmother. She is too young to know the truth and it is hard for me to tell others of Prupe and her fascination with eating kin. She is blind now and cannot see but she has a sixth sense which rivals none but is far superior. She has been turned from site to blind, like the Madhi have been turned to dingo; but you cannot change what they are within. I am on my way to see her now in order to give her food for I fear what she will do if she grows hungry."

"It is a huge burden that you have accepted," said Kalti.

"I have little choice, for her granddaughter is special to me, the last living relative I have, for Prupe has eaten all the others," said Koromarange as tears filled her eyes. "Forgive me; this is so hard for me."

"No, not at all," insisted Nalon. "Please continue, for we would like to help if we can."

"There is no way of helping," said Koromarange. "Prupe is an evil woman and deserves death but I feel so… helpless. I cannot see to her death, it is not within me to treat another so coldly. She is family, you see. She is my sister and shall be for the remainder of my time alive. So long as I breathe air I shall give aid to her, but I shall not help her to kill. The only way I have to prevent her doing evil is to keep her fed and fed well."

"I think I understand," said Nalon. "And so long as you can ensure she does no further harm then she shall remain in her present form, to eat of what you take her."

"I must go now," said Koromarange, "for she will be expecting me. Please make yourselves comfortable by my fire and rest."

"Thank you, Koromarange; we shall," said Nalon, smiling. And before she departed company he passed one more comment. "Dig and you shall reap reward." She did not fully understand this but said nothing.

Koromarange approached Prupe after having left Koakangi near a large rock not far away.

"Here, Prupe," said Koromarange. "I am here, with food."

"You are late, my sister, for I have been growing hungry," replied Prupe.

"I am sorry," said a nervous Koromarange, for she did not want her sister to know what she was hiding not so far away.

"What is it?" asked Prupe.

"Berries, yams, and some good meat from possum," said Koromarange.

"No, not that," said Prupe. "Something is the matter. I can hear it in your voice and hear it in the way you walk. You are hiding something from me, I feel it."

"That is absurd, Prupe. I have nothing to hide. I have no possessions."

"Not possession, but something else," pried Prupe. "Maybe it is a possession but... not a possession. You guard something."

"No, I do not," insisted Koromarange. "All I have is what I carry, and it is food for you. There is no burden in the things I do for you."

"But it comes at a price."

"But you know that you will be killed if others find out about you," said Koromarange.

"Yes, maybe you are right, but still, I feel as though something is the matter," said Prupe. "Come; give your sister a hug."

And so Koromarange leant forward and exchanged greeting with her sister.

"There, that wasn't so bad, was it?" said Prupe. "But I must say, that smell you wear is very strange."

"There are many people in the camp, many smells to linger and stick," said Koromarange.

"It smells familiar, like something I have known before; something I was very close to."

"It is nothing, Prupe," rushed Koromarange. "I must be getting back, quickly. I shall endeavour to be here on time tonight, to give you something else before the curtain of darkness draws over the sky."

"No need," said Prupe. "I am very tired and will sleep after I have eaten, and shall not wake until morning."

"Very well," said Koromarange. "Oh, I have something for you, a seashell necklace that I traded just the other day. I thought you might like to wear it. Here, let me put it on you."

Koromarange put the necklace upon Prupe who patted it admiringly. "Thank you."

That night, when all was quiet, Prupe crawled effortlessly along the dry ground towards the camp: her hunger drove her on and on.

Prupe could feel the warmth given off by the fires in the camp and knew exactly where she was for she had lived here most of her life. It was true that they were hunter-gatherers and wandered around, but they always came back to their most favoured piece of ground eventually.

Prupe stopped and listened, the possums in the trees, the rodents amongst the litter on the ground, and the light rustling of leaves upon the trees surrounding the camp. They were all natural sounds and ignored by members of the clan, and the noise she made as she approached was very little and nothing more than nature procured.

Eventually she came upon the hut which she was seeking. Here lay her sister, Koromarange, fast asleep and oblivious to Prupe.

Prupe stretched her hand inside the entrance to the hut and fondled around until her nimble fingers fell upon the one she was seeking. She had found Koakangi.

Prupe smiled at her discover and pulled herself back into hiding, placing leaves upon her body and remaining in place until morning. And as the sun came up the people of the camp commenced to stir. Men went hunting and Koromarange took an empty bladder in search for water.

"I shall not be long, Koakangi," said Koromarange. "Stay here and do not wander off. I shall not be long."

Koakangi smiled and fell back to sleep, her eyes were heavy and she was keen for further slumber. It was now that Prupe came out of hiding and as blind as she was she soon discovered Koakangi and took her up in her arms. With one hand held over her mouth and the other under her body, Prupe took off slowly to her own camp fire.

By the time Koromarange had returned to her hut she was utterly devastated to see that Koakangi was gone and that the ground was trodden down heavily, as though something had been dragged away across the ground. At first she considered that a dingo had taken poor Koakangi away but then she realised that Prupe must have snuck up upon her and ran away with her prize, for the necklace she had given Prupe the day before had fallen from her neck and was laying upon the ground.

She picked the necklace up, tossed it down before her hut, and raced off to face Prupe.

Koromarange had changed tactic as she approached the small camp in which Prupe called her own. She could see Prupe not far away and she was tying Koakangi to a tree.

"Please, Grandmother," pleaded Koakangi. "I did not do anything wrong. I have been very good. I have been learning to gather yams, berries, and nuts this week."

"Never fear, young one," said Prupe. "For you have done no wrong. But tie you up I must, for you are to do me a service."

"May I better serve you untied?" queried Koakangi.

"Oh, no; certainly not," cried Prupe, "for I am to eat you."

The shock on the face of Koakangi was indescribable. The fear that welled up inside her was so strong that she couldn't possibly cry.

"Eat me," said Koakangi. "But you are my grandmother."

"Yes," said Prupe. "Who else deserves to eat of your flesh than I?"

Prupe started to laugh a heinous laugh just then and wandered off, her arms outstretched before her, for she needed some firewood in order to cook her catch of the day.

Koromarange took this opportunity to approach the stricken Koakangi and as she closed the gap she indicated for Koakangi not to say a word.

Koromarange then whispered into her ear. "I shall save you, young one, but I am short on time and must be done with a single choir before Prupe returns. Say not a word and I shall untie you in time."

And with those words spoken, Koromarange began to dig a very deep hole in front of where Koakangi was tied.

Prupe took a while to find all the wood she required before returning and when she returned is was with slow and deliberate movement, for she didn't wish to be lost of her camp.

Koromarange saw her coming and fitted the last touches to her work before pleading with Koakangi in delicate tone.

"Do not let the witch know what we know. I shall be back soon enough but must now hide before she draws close enough to smell me."

"Are you still here, Koakangi?" asked Prupe, teasingly.

"Yes, grandmother," replied Koakangi. "Where else should I be."

"Did you miss your grandmother?"

"Would you tease a possum before eating it... so why tease me?"

"It is not a matter of teasing, but testing, and I am satisfied now that you are still here and ready to be cooked."

Prupe laughed a cackling laugh and felt around, feeding the dying embers of the fire she had left behind, adding tinder under a flame hot enough to burn the tips of her fingers leapt up. She then added most of the firewood she had collected and waited patiently for it to become hot with red coals and charcoal.

"Not long now, my precious, and you will be in a warm enough place," said Prupe, laughing once more. "Oh, I almost forgot."

Prupe turned and moved off to her hut to retrieve her stick which she used to test the meat of her victims before eating them, and as she rummaged through her few possessions Koromarange made good the opportunity to come out of hiding and make fast a taunt vine. When Prupe returned she tripped over the vine and fell head first into the hole which Koromarange had dug.

Prupe hang there on the precipice and below her was a stage of sharpened fangs, sticks with points pushed into the bottom. One slip from Prupe and she would be skewered like her victims.

"Help," cried Prupe. "Help me."

Koromarange came up to the lip of the deep hole which suddenly looked deeper than what she had dug. The hole she had created was nowhere near as deep as this. And then she recalled once more what Nalon had said to her: Dig and you shall reap reward. He had made the hole deeper than she had dug; by some form of magic the hole was now as deep as the tallest tree was tall. She now believed, without a doubt, that Nalon was Baiame.

"You have been sinful, Prupe," said Koromarange. "And I have been a fool to protect you. But I shall protect you no longer."

Without further word, but the cries from Prupe for aid, Koromarange released Koakangi from her bonds and both ran away from Prupe and her camp.

"I hear you running," yelled Prupe. "Come back and help your sister... come back and give aid to your grandmother, Koakangi."

Prupe struggled and felt around upon the lip of the hole. She found a stick and tried to grasp it but only managed to unsettle the fire she had made. A burning stick fell from the fire and the dry vegetation around it quickly caught light. The grass around burnt crisply and Prupe tried to shield her eyes of the heat and the flames. She fell then, to her death, upon the sharpened stakes at the bottom of the pit.

Kalti and Nalon were walking away from the clan, of which they did not know its name, when Kalti asked of Nalon: "Do you think that Prupe will meet her fate?"

Nalon considered the situation, or what he had known of it, for he did not bother to entertain a reality of what was to come of her, for it was becoming well known that evil never prospered over good.

"A fate worse than death... I do," said Nalon. "For you can change a man into a dingo, but you can never take away his sinful nature; but all bad things wither and die in the end."

"The good die too," said Kalti.

"But there is honour and truth," finished Nalon of the conversation and they continued walking without breaking stride.

170

SEPARATE WAYS

Nalon and Kalti had crossed the great expanse of the open plains when they came across an even vaster area of sparse foliage: tufts of grass, bushes, and trees of many varieties.

The creatures so created by Yowie were nowhere to be seen and it was assumed by both men that this was due to the great distance they had travelled, whereby the great herds had been left far behind them.

Nalon came to a stop and sniffed the air. He turned to Kalti. "Do you smell it?"

Kalti sniffed the air as Nalon had done before him and came back with his reply. "Yes," he said. "I smell water, and it must be a vast amount."

"We are near the sacred place," said Nalon. "We shall soon be at Tarana [large waterhole] and in its middle there is an island with but a single tree."

"A tree?" queried Kalti.

"A Yarran tree, so sacred that Yowie is sure to have cast some form of magic in order to prevent us from finding it," said Nalon.

"A tree upon an island," considered Kalti. "How hard can it be?"

"We shall see," advised Nalon as he stepped off in the right direction. "But I do not underestimate Death."

And so they continued on for some time when they fell upon the greatest body of water either of them had seen in their entire lives. The expanse of glimmering surface stretched so far that it was almost impossible to see the island at its middle, but something made it easier to see than not.

"See for yourself, Kalti," said Nalon. "Do you still think it will be easy?"

Kalti looked. "No, you are right." And there before them both they saw that the island in the distance was so covered in trees that it would be almost impossible to find what they were looking for. "Do you know what a Yarran tree looks like?"

"Not really," admitted Nalon. "And that will be our undoing; however, I can defeat this lack of knowledge."

"How?" asked Kalti, as he looked out over the great expanse of water called Tarana.

"Before I tell you I must advise of one important factor. We cannot call upon Baiame for aid. As for the remainder…. Baiame did create the sacred tree and its very essence. There is also honey within the tree, created by the honey bees which they store in their hive, a great temptation to man. Baiame said to the first created man, Ber-rook-boorn, 'the bees make it from the pollen of flowers. The honey is for them. And I should also warn you that I have placed Narahdarn, the bat, to watch over the honey which is for the bees. Narahdarn will be drawn forth if the honey is taken by you and then you will have to deal with Death.'"

"Why would Baiame create such a terrible flow of circumstances?" asked Kalti.

"To test those which he did create, to ensure that they were worthy of all his gifts," replied Nalon. "He then said to Ber-rook-boorn, 'Death has the power to take your life if my laws should be broken, and there is nothing I can do about it, although death will not be delivered by his direct hand. This tree belongs to Death as the honey belongs to the bees, all of this in the same way that the name Ber-rook-boorn now belongs to you. Do not touch the honey.'"

"It is crazy," said Kalti. "Why would Baiame create a sacred tree and then give it to Death?"

"As I have said," continued Nalon. "It was a test, a means to ensure that laws would remain sacred. If the temptations of man could be controlled by preventing him from eating the honey within the sacred tree then he could be prevented from breaking the other laws of the land. There is also something further. When the honey was taken from the tree the tree did weep. The tree cried tears of red gum which fell down the trunk of the sacred tree. The tears dried in the form of red gum."

"But the clans eat honey now," said Kalti.

"But that honey is not of the sacred tree," said Nalon. "There is a difference: call it symbolism if you wish."

"I did not know any of this," said Kalti.

"But you know now," said Nalon. "And now that you know all there is to know you must turn back and go to the other clans. Tell them everything you have learnt from me. They have forgotten the tale of the sacred tree."

"I cannot leave you," said Kalti.

"Your job is done and mine is almost complete," said Nalon. "Only I must approach the sacred tree and restore the faith which has been lost."

"I was hoping to see it all for myself: the end of the journey and the joy that it shall bring."

"The joy is in the giving," said Nalon. "And that is what you are to do. Go now and give. Give to the clans the laws of the land. The laws we have spoken of in the midst of others and at times when we were by ourselves around a warm fire. Go and share all of this knowledge and reinforce what you have learnt by teaching others."

"How shall I know that you have saved the day and restored all hope?" asked Kalti.

"You shall hear the voice of my Gayandi, for it travels far; not only this but my task is almost complete, for I have the word of Baiame swirling around inside my head."

"How shall you cross the water? How shall you find the tree? How will you do these things?"

"It is too many questions," said Nalon. "Believe in me, for aid is coming to me. No more questions now. Go, and complete your task."

"Yes, Nalon," said Kalti. "Thank you. You are a great man."

"And you are a great companion, who is worth more, for a companion can be either man or woman. To exult yourself above both sexes is a greater achievement than by being a simple man alone."

Kalti smiled and said not a further word as he turned to begin his journey back from whence they had come.

THE BUNYIP

Nalon did not wait long when a man came crashing through the reeds along the edge of Tarana. Suddenly he stopped dead in his tracks and looked up at Nalon.

"Who are you?"

"I am Nalon, and I have come to restore hope," said Nalon, with a smile. "Who are you?"

"I am Bardo [water], but most people know me as the frog man."

Nalon pursed his lips in the direction of the island. "I wish to go there."

Bardo looked. "I wish you luck."

"Can you help me?"

"Maybe I can, but first you have to tell me your story," insisted Bardo.

"A story is more easily told on a full stomach," returned Nalon.

"A story for food," said Bardo as he considered. "I have not heard a good story in a while and so I shall do this thing, but give me a moment."

Bardo stood there on the spot and looked out over the water. He looked and looked, and when he considered all to be quiet he waded into the water until he disappeared below the surface. Suddenly a small piece of vegetation exposed itself. Nalon smiled. Bardo was using the reed to breath under water. Bardo did not have to wait long when three ducks appeared swimming along towards him. With great suddenness two of the ducks disappeared beneath the surface for Bardo had grabbed onto their legs and pulled them under. Bardo returned to stand beside Nalon moments later, two ducks the richer.

"Give me some time and you will have something to eat."

Nalon looked up into the sky and considered what he was about to do. He was going to partake of flesh not meant to be eaten. But if he was to get to the island then he would have little choice.

The meal was over and Nalon had completed his story. The fire was still warm and the curtain of night had drawn. Nalon looked into the eyes of Bardo.

"That was an interesting story, Nalon," congratulated Bardo. "But now I must give one to you. Lend me your ear and you shall learn of my misfortune."

"Please," insisted Nalon. "I shall not interrupt you as you did not interrupt me."

"Firstly I wish to ask something of you. Do you know of the creature called bunyip?"

"I have seen this creature but know little of it, other than the fact that it is a creation of Yowie."

"If that is the case then I am more inclined to give you aid, for the story you have told me, although hard to believe in parts, is understood and largely accepted. Do not ask me why but there is something about you which fills me with trust. Anyway, I shall tell you now of my wife. I was taking ducks from the water, as I did today, when the bunyip appeared behind me. My wife called warning and I tried to hand her the ducks and scramble safely from the reeds, the water, and the mud. Before I knew it, however, the bunyip was upon me, but instead of taking me he snatched onto the arm of my wife and took her instead.

"I was devastated.

"That night I took a spear and captured many frogs. I tied the frogs upside-down to the spear and left them there amongst the reeds. The next morning the frogs were all dead and the bunyip had not shown itself. So I did the same again and the next morning the frogs were gone. Their croaking had drawn the bunyip to them and he fed upon their flesh. I did this for a further five nights before I caught a glimpse of the bunyip, for I had closed the gap between me and the spear so finely that I could not miss it; the reeds were so thick it was hard to see, even with the full moon

"I was lucky I was not seen myself. But I made myself appear before him for upon his back was my wife. She was in a trance and would not look at me from upon the shoulders of the bunyip. The bunyip ignore me as he had eaten quickly, and I can only assume, as my wife was with him, that he had no more room for further burden.

"He was as you had explained; very hideous, and he stuck me with terror.

"He disappeared and I waded in behind him. As it was a full moon I could just make out the head of my wife, gliding across the top of the water. They were headed for the island. The bunyip was very fast and so I returned to the bank of Tarana. The next day I made a raft and paddled out to the island. I thought that the bunyip might be nocturnal and hoped this to be true. When I came upon the island it was hard to move anywhere for it was so thick with trees, but after a lengthy search I heard buzzing. I was drawn to it, but no matter how hard I looked I could not find where the buzzing came from. I came back here to consider my next move for the last thing I wished to do was stay on the island for fear of the bunyip.

"That is my story, Nalon."

"I am sorry to hear of your wife but maybe I can help," said Nalon, the brows upon the head of Bardo shifting upwards as though intrigued. "I could tell you more stories but think it unnecessary. I know a trick that will get us to the beehive for I know this to be the location of the sacred tree of which I seek. The bunyip is nothing more than a manipulation of the Yowie. You must take me to your raft, Bardo, as soon as the sun comes up in the morning. This will give us plenty of time to get to the island."

The following morning Bardo did as he knew he should. Nalon was going to help him find his wife and Bardo was going to help Nalon find the sacred tree.

They rowed out to the island and by the time the sun was high above them they had stepped foot upon hard ground.

"You are right, Bardo," said Nalon. "This is very thick."

"Yes," agreed Bardo. "Now I have brought you here how do you propose to find the tree and my wife?"

"I believe both to be at the one location. We seek a tree that has a beehive in it, which has large blobs of red gum upon it." Nalon looked around. "There," he pursed his lips. "I see a spider in a tree. Let us go to it."

They walked over and Bardo watched carefully as Nalon took from it several lengths of spider thread.

"Now all we need is a bee," said Nalon.

They moved over to a bush which was full of blossom and waited. They waited and waited until after a short time they saw a bee approach. As the bee landed upon a flower of the bush, Nalon took the bee in between two fingers and the placed the spiders web around one of its legs. Nalon next let the bee go and with the other end of the spider thread in his hand was lead towards the centre of the island.

Bardo was so pleased with what was happening that he remained in stunned silence the whole time.

It was not long before they both heard the buzzing of the hive, and releasing the bee of its bonds they watched where it went and quickly followed.

They moved around a rock and stopped dead in their tracks, for their before them was the sacred yarran tree. On the other side of the tree Bardo could see his wife. She was petrified as though made of wood.

"My beautiful wife," yelled Bardo as he raced towards her with outstretched arms, and as he stepped to within just a short distance of the tree he too, turned to petrified wood, his arms reaching for his wife in silence.

Nalon simply looked on. He had known something was the matter when he saw the wife. Now they were both petrified.

"I know you are near, for I can feel your presence," said Nalon. "Come out so that I can see you."

"You come to the tree," said the bunyip, hidden from view. "Come into the shade of the yarran tree and be cast into a perpetual state of wood."

Nalon heard the voice and stepped towards the tree. He walked right up to it and saw the globs of red gum upon the trunk.

"What is the manner of this… you have not been petrified," said the voice of the bunyip.

"That is because I am the true representation of Baiame, and I cannot fall beneath a simple curse, neither cast by you or Death."

"But… but…. This cannot be," said the bunyip.

"And you shall see more, even clearly if you were to come out of hiding."

"The sun is still up and whilst I can see my shadow I must remain in hiding."

"I shall create a storm soon enough and you can come out then," said Nalon. "I do not mind."

Nalon lifted his arms to the air and gave a command. A thunderstorm suddenly appeared and a flash of lightning struck out at the earth. Both of the petrified figures of man and wife were torn from their bonds and reborn of their flesh. They hugged each other and moved away from the tree, arm in arm. The bunyip, however, remained hidden.

Bardo stopped to look at Nalon. "Thank you for what you have done."

Nalon did not know what it was he had done but he was ever thankful.

"No," said Nalon. "I must thank you, for without your aid I would never have made it this far. But remember one thing for the future. Always keep the bunyip well fed, for with plenty to eat he will not cast his magic trance upon the people, and he will have no reason to store them in a petrified state in storage for when he is without food."

"Do you think that is what he meant for us; for us to be eaten when he was ready?" asked Bardo.

"Yes, that is exactly what he wished."

Bardo and his wife continued on as they walked off. Bardo then stopped and turned again. "Are you not coming?"

"No," replied Nalon.

"Then how will you get off the island?"

'I shall find my own way shortly, you need not help me further, but at present I need some time alone, but before you go remember this: never seek the shade of the yarran tree, for it is sacred; and always be sure to leave plenty of food within Tarana, or the bunyip shall come looking for you once more."

Bardo simply nodded and was on his way.

When the other two had gone Nalon turned his attention once more to the bunyip who was hidden. "You did not show yourself, or let the others know of your presence. Is it fear?"

"I have no fear," said the bunyip.

"That is true and untrue, for what is to fear but fear itself?" replied Nalon. "Come out and show yourself."

"I shall not," said the bunyip. "I shall be gone soon enough, but I tell you this one thing. I shall return and eat the flesh of your kin, for that stupid man and his wife will forget to leave the food of Tarana for me and me alone. They will harvest the waters as they have always done and then I shall go swimming after them."

Nalon stretched his hands out then and held them against the yarran, his palms covering the tears of red gum.

"What is it you are doing?" asked the bunyip.

"I am healing old wounds," replied Nalon, and as the bunyip watched he could see the tears of red gum dry up and disappear as Nalon gave forgiveness to the wife of Ber-rook-boorn for what she had done. The yarran tree and Nalon had come to terms; the sacred tree had been made sacred once more.

"I say to you this thing, bunyip," said Nalon. "I know your maker and I have a message for him. This yarran tree shall always be sacred and never again shall man nor woman take from it the essence which makes it so. The laws are being restored and with

180

them the race of men and women cast by Baiame will live on forever. They shall cleanse the land of the burna-korra, mallee-akana, wonambi, kyeema, pindoola and thylacoleo; all the evil created by his wicked hand, and by the hand of Marmoo, but some things will be kept in the balance, to give aid to the people in their life, such as the insects which feed the beautiful birds of this world. Now be gone with you."

Nalon listened. Not a stirring could be heard. As though by magic the bunyip had disappeared, but Nalon held no doubt within him that the bunyip would return to be a menace in the future.

Nalon felt exhausted but he had accomplished what he had set out to do. He had completed his walkabout, he had established a history, a history which would be known as dreamtime, for dreamtime was eternal and the laws of the land were a part of it for all time.

Nalon sat down beneath the yarran tree and rested.

THE GIFT

Nalon woke up; he was seated beneath the yarran tree. Nalon lifted his eyes as Baiame appeared before him. Baiame then sat opposite Nalon.

"You have achieved a miracle," said Baiame. "I thank you."

"Should you even be here, Baiame? What if Yowie was to hear of this and come calling, to create further havoc?"

"No, he will not come now. The yarran tree has been returned to its former essence, it is sacred once more. Let us hope that no one will come here again and tempt the vigour of Death."

There was silence then and Baiame looked deep into the eyes of Nalon. "You have done a great deed and shall be rewarded."

"I have one request, and that will be reward enough."

"Speak it," commanded Baiame.

"Kira and Kala went towards the coast. They have tempted my fury by disobeying laws, for the laws exist upon the land and should not be broken."

"Ah," said Baiame. "I grant you this, that that will be attended to. I shall turn them into pillars of stone once they reach the coast, for that is where they are heading. That is the least I can do for you. But I shall do more than just simply tricks, for you have earned a place in eternity."

"Eternity; that is a long time," stated Nalon.

"When next I cast my magic you shall be transformed into a star, the brightest within the night. The first star to be seen at night and the last star to disappear in morning. Whenever anyone looks up at the night sky they shall see you and remember all you have done."

"There is no fear in that," said Nalon.

"Fear; of course there is no fear," said Baiame. "You will be a wondrous sight."

"But your creations of all men and women will not remember the laws. They will not recall the dreamtime nor see favour in conducting walkabout. They will all forget unless fear is present, but they will always fear that which is fearsome."

"Are you saying that you do not wish to be a star?" asked Baiame.

"I would love to be a star," said Nalon, "as created by you, a reminder of all I have done in your name, but I also see that fear needs to be invoked within the people."

"How would you propose to do that?"

"A monster demon, one who is so loathsome and evil, that Yowie and Marmoo will be forgotten. You shall call him yara-ma-yha-who and all will fear him."

"Yes," agreed Baiame. "That will be fear. You have done another great service to all creation."

"The legend of yara-ma-yha-who shall be my last gift to the people. I shall lay visit to Kalti and others that I have come to trust in the past. The legend will strike fear into all those that hear his name, and dreamtime will be eternal."

Baiame bent down and picked up a stone and handed this to Nalon. "Go and do what you need to do. Use my Gayandi if you need to, or visit each in person: or simply visit them each in their dreams. Once you have completed you task you shall cast this stone upon the ground and I shall turn you into a star."

"To secure fear within them; for them to form an eternal idea; for dreamtime and walkabout to be as a part of the land as the people themselves; to have this delivered to them in a dream. It is a wonderful idea and it shall be done," said Nalon. "I shall do this thing and live the remainder of my life in the night sky, to bear witness to dreamtime, for ever and ever."

YARA-MA-YHA-WHO

The old women known as Ghera [a gum leaf] sat at the fire, the children surrounding it and listening with great intent.

"It is time to remind you, children, of yara-ma-yha-who," said Ghera.

The children all reached out for the comfort of the others around them, fear painted over their faces, each child looking over their shoulders both left and right.

"He will be after you if you are naughty," said Ghera. "You must always abide by the laws of dreamtime, for it is eternal, and if you wish to live an eternal existence after death then you must be sure to listen and learn."

"Why does yara-ma-yha-who only eat children?" asked Cardinia [the dawn], a young girl of just six years.

"To put fear into the adults," replied Ghera. "So that the adults, too, will never forget that dreamtime is eternal. No mother or father would wish to see their child eaten. This is the strongest fear."

"But the brightest star in the night sky will watch over us," said Taree [a wild fig], a young boy of seven years.

"This is sometimes true," said Ghera. "But on nights when Yowie casts a net over the sky; what then?"

"The star will not be seen," answered Cardinia. "It will not be able to see us or protect us."

"You must all remember, children that the brightest star in the night sky will help protect you from yara-ma-yha-who, but Death will always be lingering to see injustice done. So long as we live by the eternal laws of dreamtime, we shall always be sheltered from harm."

CPSIA information can be obtained
at www.ICGtesting.com
Printed in the USA
LVOW04s1152270116

472173LV00034B/744/P